MW00648033
Bottom-Tier
CHARACTER
TOMOZAKI
YUKI YAKU
Illustration by
Fly
The Masked Pilot and the Fairy of Truth

Hanging out by the river

"Don't
let go..."

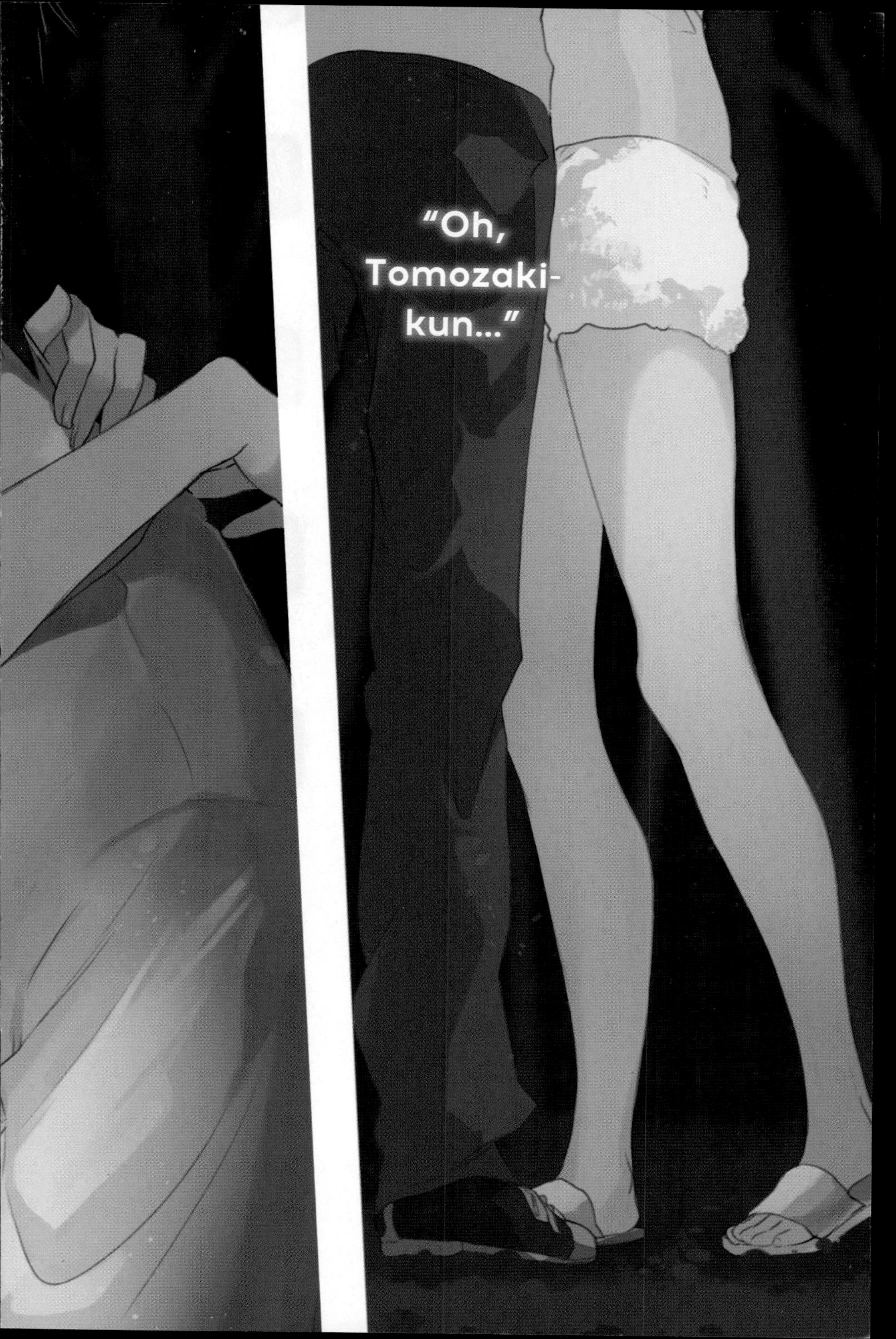
"Oh,
Tomozaki-
kun..."

"It's so beautiful, isn't it...?"

The colorful
fireworks
blossomed in
the dark sky.

Bottom-Tier Character Tomozaki, Level 3

CONTENTS

Takei

Design Yuko Mucadeya + Caiko Monma (musicagographics)

Bottom-Tier
CHARACTER
TOMOZAKI
Lv.3
Yuki Yaku
Illustration by Fly
The Masked Pilot and the ★★★ Fairy of Truth
YEN ON
New York

Bottom-Tier Character Tomozaki Lv.3

YUKI YAKU

Cover art by Fly
Translation by Winifred Bird

JAKU CHARA TOMOZAKI-KUN LV.3
by Yuki YAKU

Illustration by FLY

Original Japanese edition published by SHOGAKUKAN.
English translation rights in the United States of America, Canada, the United Kingdom, Ireland, Australia, and New Zealand arranged with SHOGAKUKAN through Tuttle-Mori Agency, Inc.

Yen On
150 West 30th Street, 19th Floor
New York, NY 10001

Visit us at yenpress.com
facebook.com/yenpress
twitter.com/yenpress
yenpress.tumblr.com
instagram.com/yenpress

First Yen On Edition: March 2020

Yen On is an imprint of Yen Press, LLC.
The Yen On name and logo are trademarks of Yen Press, LLC.

Library of Congress Cataloging-in-Publication Data
Names: Yaku, Yuki, author. | Fly, 1963- illustrator. | Bird, Winifred, translator.
Title: Bottom-tier character Tomozaki / Yuki Yaku ; illustration by Fly ; translation by Winifred Bird.
Other titles: Jyakukyara Tomozaki-kun. English
Description: First Yen On edition. | New York : Yen On, 2019-
Identifiers: LCCN 2019017466 | ISBN 9781975358259 (v. 1 : pbk.) | ISBN 9781975384586 (v. 2 : pbk.) | ISBN 9781975384593 (v. 3 : pbk.)
Subjects: LCSH: Video games—Fiction. | Video gamers—Fiction.
Classification: LCC PL877.5.A35 J9313 2019 | DDC 895.63/6-dc23
LC record available at https://lccn.loc.gov/2019017466

ISBNs: 978-1-9753-8459-3 (paperback)
978-1-9753-8642-9 (ebook)

10 9 8 7 6 5 4 3 2 1

LSC-C

Printed in the United States of America

Lv.3

Bottom-Tier Character Tomozaki

Fumiya Tomozaki
Second-year high school student. Bottom-tier.

Aoi Hinami
Second-year high school student. Perfect heroine of the school.

Minami Nanami
Second-year high school student. Class clown.

Hanabi Natsubayashi
Second-year high school student. Small.

Yuzu Izumi
Second-year high school student. Hot.

Fuka Kikuchi
Second-year high school student. Bookworm.

Takahiro Mizusawa
Second-year high school student. Wants to be a beautician.

Shuji Nakamura
Second-year high school student. Class boss.

Takei
Second-year high school student. Built.

Tsugumi Narita
First-year high school student. Easygoing.

Common Honorifics

In order to preserve the authenticity of the Japanese setting of this book, we have chosen to retain the honorifics used in the original language to express the relationships between characters.

No honorific: Indicates familiarity or closeness; if used without permission or reason, addressing someone in this manner would constitute an insult.

-san: The Japanese equivalent of Mr./Mrs./Miss. If a situation calls for politeness, this is the fail-safe honorific.

-kun: Used most often when referring to boys, this indicates affection or familiarity. Occasionally used by older men among their peers, but it may also be used by anyone referring to a person of lower standing.

-chan: An affectionate honorific indicating familiarity used mostly in reference to girls; also used in reference to cute persons or animals of either gender.

-senpai: An honorific indicating respect for a senior member of an organization. Often used by younger students with their upperclassmen at school.

1

When you go back to the starter town with the full party, new stuff tends to happen

It was the first day of summer vacation—although the break wasn't going to be much of a break for me.

"Typical. You showed up in a ridiculous outfit."

It was eleven in the morning, and as soon as I arrived at the standard meetup spot by the Bean Tree sculpture in Omiya Station, I was in trouble. Naturally, only one person would be so critical and yet so matter-of-fact.

Aoi Hinami, the perfect heroine of our school and my teacher in life.

"B-be quiet."

"Pfft. So you know how bad you look?" she said in an extremely haughty tone, crossing her arms.

"Uhhh..."

What with Mimimi's student council campaign and our lack of communication after that, I hadn't heard much of Hinami's sharp tongue in the recent lead-up to vacation. Once I got over being offended, however, I realized the old Hinami was back in full force. Her unyielding willingness to shred my self-confidence made me feel like we'd never been apart.

"Is that supposed to be your attempt at improvement?"

"I—I guess so..."

Completely defeated, I glanced down at my outfit. It wasn't the one I'd bought off the mannequin with her. I was wearing a well-worn T-shirt with some mysterious English phrase on it over a pair of knee-length jean shorts I'd gotten in junior high. In other words, stuff I'd gotten ages ago with my parents at a cheap department store. At least my shoes were the ones I'd gotten recently as part of that other outfit.

"Well, I certainly can't see any sign of it."

"I did think about this outfit…"

If you're wondering why I didn't just wear the mannequin outfit, that's because it had long sleeves and long pants, so it was too hot for summer.

"Sheesh. It looks like I'm going to have to give you a special assignment for this…"

Ignoring my excuse, she rested her thumb on her lips, deep in thought. The instant a new problem arose, she started to work on a solution. Her usual Spartan approach was in high gear—for Hinami, summer vacation wasn't a vacation. Of course, the root of the problem was my horrible fashion sense, but I'd rather not dwell on that.

"No, I mean, those clothes we bought before are way too hot…so I didn't think I should wear them."

I wasn't confident, but I told her what I was thinking anyway. I might have gotten away with the pants, but a long-sleeve shirt was out of the question. I figured she'd be even angrier if I wore that, so I went with this instead. Guess I should have at least worn the pants. I had to admit that compared to the mannequin outfit, this was straight out of junior high. Even I could tell I looked awkward. After she'd said something anyway.

"True. If you'd worn that outfit, that would have been even worse. But that doesn't make this one okay," she deadpanned without a trace of polite restraint. Although she wasn't completely deadpan—I glimpsed a faintly sadistic smile as she made her blunt point. This was why I couldn't let my guard down with her. Everything about her self-presentation was beyond perfect, yet her sadistic side would rear its head at the most random-seeming times.

"Still the same Hinami…"

"Let me guess. Your sewing kit in elementary school had a dragon design on it, right?"

My heart skipped a beat. I remembered we'd gotten to choose from a bunch of different options, and sure enough, I'd chosen the dragon on a black background. I'd picked it because it was cool. I mean, come on. It was a dragon.

"Why…? What does that have to do with anything?"

"Nerdy types instinctively tend to choose that one. We have to start by getting rid of that instinct. It's not cool."

"Nerdy types..."

For one brief, foolish second, I took comfort in the thought that the old Hinami was back, and that was my first mistake. If she kept hitting the nail on the head over and over, I'd be reduced to a blubbering mess.

"Well, let's not worry about that for the moment. I called you here to talk about something more important."

"Let's not worry about the fact that you just shredded my self-confidence?"

Hinami ignored my weak attempt at a comeback and kept talking. Yeah, same old Hinami. "So far, you've been out with me a number of times, you've been drawn into normie circles, and you spent a lot of one-on-one time with Mimimi. You've stocked up a lot of EXP, but you still don't know how to act on a date, do you?"

"Um, well..." I mean, I'd never been on a date, so...

"Pretty soon, that's going to become necessary, right? General date training, I mean."

"Pretty soon? Uh, I'm not planning on it..."

Hinami sighed with exasperation. Yes, this was familiar. "Listen. What's the minor goal you're currently supposed to be aiming for? Or did you forget?"

"...Oh right." Belatedly, I remembered. We'd been over it a million times. "I'm supposed to go out alone with a girl other than you...right?"

Hinami nodded tiredly. "In other words...," she prompted.

"...Date training is extremely necessary."

Grinning, Hinami pointed at me in a grown-up way. "Hexactly."

There it was. So we were back to the daily grind of training.

"Okay, okay," I said, nodding slightly. "You're right."

And that's how my summer vacation quickly became more work, thanks to my dependably Spartan teacher. I guess NO NAME, with her terrifyingly efficient use of time, was making her presence known. Well, once things got to this point, my only option was to dive in.

"Okay, then. Let's get some lunch and go over the details," she said, as if that was the obvious next step.

"Let me guess, you want something with che— Ow!"

She kicked me midsentence.

* * *

"…Ah, so good!"

Hinami smiled, clearly in a good mood thanks to her pasta at the Western-style restaurant in a shopping arcade outside the east exit of Omiya Station. She'd ordered the gorgonzola cream sauce. My hamburger lunch set was damn good, too.

"So what does this general date training entail exactly?" I asked.

Hinami paused her blissful chewing and swallowed the bite of pasta. "Today we'll go to a bunch of stores, and I'll give you assignments in each one."

"Uh, what kind of assignments…?"

"Well…"

She took another bite of pasta. Her smile was a little more restrained this time, maybe because she realized I was watching her. *Too late.*

She swallowed. "Simply put, we're going to rehearse for a date. I'll tell you all the places I want to go, and based on that, I want you to lead me around like you planned everything yourself."

Like I'd planned it myself?

"Um, so basically, I'll fake it?"

"Right. Even if you're just acting, I want you to practice taking the lead on a date. Just one round of practice can make a huge difference."

"Just acting…"

"Based on the information I'm about to give you, I want you to say things like, *Hey, mind if we stop in here?* or whatever. You're going to pull me along."

Ah. So that's what she meant. The idea made me a little nervous, but if I was just acting, I could do it. That feeling was probably a sign of overconfidence.

"Okay…got it."

"Great. This is what I had in mind."

Hinami did something on her phone, and mine buzzed. She'd sent me the names of three stores and their websites on LINE.

"Uh, this is where we're going today?"

"Right." Somehow, she was easy to understand even with a mouthful of pasta.

Hey, wait, why're we going here? "I mean, the first and third ones make sense…a clothing store and Starbucks, right?"

"Yeah. First, we'll go take care of that dorky outfit; then we'll go to Starbucks, and I'll give you another assignment."

"Oh…"

"Another assignment"—she'd said it so casually. Shuddering, I stared at my phone. The first thing on the list was the name Lazy Blue and a link. I tapped it, and the website of a clothing store near Omiya's west exit popped up. So we were going shopping there. The third item on the list simply said Starbucks. But as I read the second item, I frowned.

"Um…why are we going to Big Camera?"

The list specified it was the Big Camera in the SOGO building at the Omiya west exit, along with the Web address.

"They have a demo setup," she said grumpily.

"…And?"

Hinami glared at me before repeating the words very clearly.

"I said, a demo setup. Don't you want to play live sometimes, not just online? Without the lag? They have *Atafami*."

"Oh, okay, really? You sure do—"

I stopped midsentence. Maybe because she was mad, her cheeks were a little flushed. She always got really emotional when *Atafami* came up. In which case, I'd better not make a big deal over it. Let sleeping dogs lie. But man, she sure loves *Atafami*.

"What?" She was glaring at me.

"N-nothing. Never mind."

She glanced down for a second, like she was thinking, before smiling teasingly at me.

"…What?"

"You didn't notice?"

"Huh?"

She pointed at my face in a vaguely cruel way. "Last time we went to a clothing store you were super nervous, but this time you didn't even flinch at the idea. You sure must be relaxed if you have time to worry about going to Big Camera."

"Oh..." I saw her point. Now that she mentioned it, I realized I wasn't even scared.

"Well? All those long conversations with Mimimi and Yuzu and Mizusawa and other normies got you a ton of EXP, didn't it?"

I stared at my palms. The result of my EXP must be...

"I guess...I leveled up."

As I searched for the right words, Hinami nodded in satisfaction. "Do you remember? When you first started training with me, I said it was important for you to be able to do things on instinct, right?"

"...Yeah, I guess you did."

"In light of that, what do you think about the current situation?"

My terror of clothing shops had faded, and I hadn't even noticed. "Umm, I'm not sure how to put it..." I looked away from Hinami. "Okay~. You got a point."

Avoiding a direct answer out of shyness, I copied Izumi's "Okay."

Hinami looked into my eyes gravely, then broke into a grin. "Nicely done." Her smile was kind, with a grown-up warmth. Like an older sister grinning girlishly. The contradiction caught me off guard; I wish she'd take it easy with the surprise attacks.

"Oh, um, thanks."

I was totally embarrassed by that charming expression. She watched my reaction, looking satisfied. *Wait a second... Is this her revenge for my comment about Big Camera?*

After we finished eating, the conversation shifted to bigger goals.

"Before we start on today's assignment, I'd like to decide what you'll be doing over summer vacation."

"Like the whole break?"

"Yes," she said, looking serious. "If you work hard over the summer, you can really pull ahead of everyone else."

"You sound like a college prep teacher," I commented, then waited for her next words.

"We'll set some goals before the first day is over."

"Goals, huh?"

That sounded about right, given Hinami's usual approach.

"Yes. Your current minor goal is to go out alone with a girl other than me. From there, we'll set some other goals for you to achieve by the end of August."

"That's a little over a month from now..."

We had just over one month for summer vacation, and I had a sneaking suspicion it was about to be stuffed with assignments from Hinami.

"Given your current status and thinking realistically..."

"...Yeah?"

I nodded. *Realistically, huh?*

She may get sadistic at key moments, but when it came to the all-important assignments, she never asked me to do things that were beyond my abilities at that particular moment, as long as I exerted a little effort. It was always things like talking to a girl or asking someone to connect on LINE. I guess the point of the mini-assignments was partly to give me little successes and keep my motivation up, so there wouldn't be any point in making them impossible.

Just as I thought I was starting to understand her logic, however, she blew all my reasoning away.

"Your goal for the summer is to date Kikuchi-san."

For a moment, there was silence.

"What?!" I screeched, and Hinami glanced around. I felt like we'd done this before at a different restaurant.

"...Keep your voice down. Didn't you understand what I said?"

"I-it's not that..."

Flustered, I met her gaze. As usual, she was smiling sadistically.

"Okay, I'll say it again in simple terms. I want you, Tomozaki-kun, and Fuka Kikuchi-chan to become boyfriend and girlfriend this—"

"You don't have to spell it out…!!" I managed to keep my voice down, but my emotions were exploding. "Where do you get off calling that realistic…?!"

Hinami pouted and made a deliberately innocent face. "Where? Well, let's see. You already like her, and you're both into those Andi books, and you've already agreed to go see that movie together sometime. You have a whole month of summer vacation ahead of you. You'll have tons of chances to ask her out to do more stuff. And you're telling me it's not realistic to go from there to dating?"

"No, it's just…"

I might not agree with some of the details, but when she laid it all out objectively like that and gave me that no-excuses stare, I couldn't help admitting she was right. *S-so this is what it feels like to be brainwashed.*

"It's just…we haven't even exchanged contact info yet…"

"You mean this?" She shoved her phone in my face. Fuka Kikuchi's LINE page was displayed on the screen.

"U-uh, yeah…"

I should have guessed she was connected to everyone in our class on LINE. She snorted triumphantly. Honestly, though, wasn't she ignoring the feelings of the two people most directly involved?

"Anyway, your first assignment is to make a date with Fuka-chan to see that movie and go from there. I want you to develop your relationship until you're ready to be a couple. That's it."

"That's it? Sounds like more than enough to me."

Even as I said those words, I felt like I was dissociating a little, like my brain was running away from the situation. A second later, I realized something else.

"Wait a second. Did you just say, 'your first assignment'?"

Hinami giggled fearlessly. "You're getting sharper, I see. As you guessed, you're going to be flooded with assignments this summer."

"Flooded…?"

I pressed one hand against my forehead, but I'd half given in already.

This was going to be a summer of intensive training. Summer school from hell.

"As for the other assignments, well…" Hinami rested her pointer finger gently on her lips. "I'll just say plans for an overnight trip are in the works."

"An overnight trip?!"

"Keep your voice down." She poked my cheek crossly.

"Ouch!"

"The overnight trip would be a real godsend, but I'm still setting it up. Whether a total loser like you will be accepted in the group all depends on me. But believe me, I'm up to the challenge."

Hinami cracked her knuckles. *Why does this stuff mean so much to you?* Then again, if she put her mind to it, I was sure she'd be able to get me in somehow. I might as well consider this plan a done deal. But…

"Wh-who else is going…?" I asked timidly.

Hinami tilted her head, but I'm pretty sure she was faking. "Huh?"

That was all she said. Her playful smile and sadistically glittering eyes made me think she was planning to spring it all on me once everything was decided, just to mess with me. In which case, any questions now were basically a waste of time. I resigned myself to accepting whatever happened.

"I-I'll start preparing myself mentally for this…"

"Good idea," she said, nodding with satisfaction. "Aside from that, I have some other ideas…"

"More?" I instinctively shrank away from her.

"But I suppose I'll have to wait and see how you're doing at the end of our date today."

"Da—?!"

"Excuse me, check please!" she brightly called to the waiter, cutting off my expression of surprise.

"Yes, ma'am!"

In the moment before the waiter came over to our table, she threw me a glance that was as predictably sadistic and wicked as ever.

I'll be damned if I let this kind of thing get to me. I mean it.

* * *

We left the restaurant.

"That was so good!"

Was the date rehearsal starting now? For some reason, as soon as we stepped outside, she switched from the practical perfectionist I knew so well to the perfect heroine of our school.

"Uh, yeah." I just decided to go along with it.

She smiled brightly as we walked along side by side. "Where to next?" She locked her hands behind her back, leaned forward, and looked up at my face. *What's with the girlish pose?*

I suspected I'd be in trouble if I looked straight at her, so I shifted my gaze away. "Um, Hinami?"

Even though I was nervous about the weird situation, I finally managed to say something. *It's rehearsal, just a rehearsal.*

"Yesss?"

My nerves ramped up a gear at her fake-teasing tone.

Uh...what do I say now?

She elbowed me as if to say *Come on, what?* as I hesitated.

"N-nothing." I fired myself up again. "There's somewhere I want to go if it's okay with you."

"Sure, where?"

I suppressed the urge to say, *You're the one who decided in the first place!*

"A clothing store by the west exit."

"Oh, cool! Is it in the Arche building?"

"Y-yeah, there!"

That was definitely part of the address listed on the website she'd sent me. Was this a test to make sure I'd actually looked at the address?

"Okay, awesome!" She nodded enthusiastically, then gazed at me without moving.

...Um?

I waited for a minute to see what she would do, then belatedly realized what she was up to. *Oh right.* I was supposed to take the lead today. *O-okay, here goes.* Switching roles with Hinami felt weird, but I managed to open my mouth.

"Okay, then...let's head over there."

I started walking. She nodded girlishly and sidled up right next to me with fast, short steps. *Oh shit, she almost brushed against me just now.*

"Uh, we're here."

Using my phone to navigate, I'd led Hinami around to the classy-looking Arche building at the west exit of Omiya Station. It was weird how different everything looked when I was heading toward our destination myself instead of following someone else. If we got lost, it would be my fault. I was conscious of how my own decisions affected our progress and all the responsibility that entailed.

I'd felt a sense of responsibility when we went to buy a present for Nakamura and Hinami gave me the assignment of pushing through some of my own proposals, but this was a magnified version of that. Her assignments were definitely getting harder.

"Looks like they have a lot of cool stuff here."

She looked around, pretending to be entertained by it all. The narrow passageway was lined with women's clothing stores and packed with young people. About eight out of ten were female. *Huh? Did I come to the wrong place?* I anxiously checked the map again, but it definitely looked like the store was on the fifth floor of this building.

"U-uh, yeah. Um, the place I want to go is on the fifth floor."

"Okay! Are there stairs or something?"

She stared around with fake helplessness. I was ready to bet she knew where the escalators and elevators were. *Okay, okay, I get it—I'm supposed to take the lead once again.*

"...Um, over here?"

I made a guess and started walking with Hinami at my heels. I wasn't sure I was going in the right direction, but since there was pretty much just the one passageway, it thankfully brought me to an escalator.

"Whew." Sighing with relief, I stepped onto the escalator. It was surprisingly exhausting to take the lead, even if all I had to do was find an escalator. *Should I try to make conversation now?* As I was mulling this over, Hinami nodded and looked up at my face.

"You sure are on top of things, Tomozaki-kun!" she said energetically. I was a little startled by her praise. Oh geez, she really did have me in the palm of her hand.

* * *

Glancing at the mirror next to the narrow escalator, I caught sight of my sorry self.

"All right." Hinami had dropped the heroine act and was speaking normally again; I was probably in for another explanation. "You still only know how to buy the whole mannequin, right? That's fine if you just want to camouflage your outermost shell, but as we've seen today, when people without taste buy their own clothes, the results can be tragic," she deadpanned, sweeping her hand to indicate my reflection in the mirror.

"Was it really necessary to call me tragic?" I wiped a bead of sweat off my cheek, which was freezing thanks to the air-conditioning in the building, and mustered up my scrawny pride. *Give me back the other Hinami already!*

"Well, tell me what you think when you look in the mirror."

The guy in the mirror had a proper hairdo, a natural smile, tamed eyebrows, and a straight back. Compared to the old me, he wasn't quite such a freak, but I had to admit he looked fairly nerdy. And that it was the fault of a pretty uncool outfit.

"You can sense it yourself, can't you? That something is off?"

"I—I guess…" Although I couldn't put into words what that "something" was, I could see the nerdiness.

"At the very least, you need to buy clothes for every season."

"For every season?" I muttered, thinking about the contents of my wallet. "Being a normie is tough, isn't it…?"

Maybe Hinami guessed my line of thinking, because her next words were somewhat reassuring.

"Not that you have to buy the whole mannequin each time."

"Really?"

As a spark of hope lit up my eyes, Hinami glanced toward the top of the escalator.

"Basically, as long as you go shopping with someone who has good taste, all you need to do is buy a simple top to go with the bottom we bought before. Maybe just a T-shirt."

"Bottom?"

I had a feeling she meant something other than what I was picturing.

"Before you make any snarky comments, I'm referring to the pants," she said with a bit of disgust.

Uh, so…apparently bottom *is a word some normies will use for pants. I guess?* While I was internally wincing at that, I noticed Hinami's smile becoming increasingly sadistic.

She paused for a moment before seeming to realize she needed to add something.

"Although given how patently nerdy your current outfit is, you need to be a lot more careful. What do you think the people in the store will think when they see you?"

"C-come on, I was just starting to build up a little self-confidence!"

As I looked down once again at my outfit, the familiar dread of clothing stores welled up inside me. *Yup. Terrifying.*

The fear must have made me clumsy, because I almost stumbled as I stepped off the elevator.

"That's why I'm going to do you a special favor today…and choose your clothes for you."

Once again, I was caught off guard by her little head tilt. It was so cute it pissed me off. *No fair switching back to heroine mode all of a sudden.*

"Oh…okay." Taking the lead again, I made my way to the clothing store.

The place even smelled fashionable somehow.

"Hmm, what would look good on you? Hey, why don't you pick something out, too?"

With that, she chose two tops and I chose one, so I ended up buying three new T-shirts. According to heroine-mode Hinami, "I picked out two that will go with the pants you already have! This way you don't need to buy a new bottom! The one you chose isn't half-bad, either!"

Why does she insist on calling it a bottom*…? Why is that word necessary? I think I'm just gonna stick with* pants.

* * *

We left the store, new T-shirts in hand. As I sadly inspected my lightened wallet, Hinami rested her finger gently on her lips and started to think about something. Her eyes were on the bag hanging from my shoulder.

"...What?"

"Nothing. I was just thinking you should probably take this," she said, still in heroine mode, as she pulled a folded-up black backpack out of her own. It was simple and undecorated, the kind of thing I'd imagine university students carrying around. It looked unisex as well.

"Huh?"

"You don't have a nice backpack, do you?"

She held it out to me. I wasn't sure what to do, but I took it.

"You don't mind lending it to me?"

"Just consider it a present, okay?"

That caught me by surprise "No, no way! I mean...you've already given me too many things. First, you gave me those masks, and I still have your voice recorder..."

"Well, that's true," she said, glancing at the backpack. "But look at this. It got stuck on something sharp and tore a little, see?"

I took a closer look. Like she said, the fabric in the upper left corner was torn and fraying.

"But that's barely..."

"It bothers *me*!" she snapped. Well, it wouldn't bother me, but I guess even a little tear was unforgivable for a perfect heroine.

"But..."

When I hesitated, Hinami made a proposal. "There's an accessory store near here with something I've been wanting for a while. Why don't you buy it for me? Then we can just trade!"

Her eyes were sparkling. She seemed so nice—on the surface, that is.

It really was a good idea, though. I'd feel much better giving her something in return. But what could she possibly want? Cheese and video games were the only things I knew she liked. Wonder what it was?

"Okay, I'm in. Let's go."

Partly out of curiosity, I went along with Hinami to another building near the west exit of Omiya Station.

* * *

"Here it is!" Hinami said excitedly, still keeping up the heroine act.

We were in a busy shop that sold all sorts of stuff, from clothes and hats to rings and cell phone covers. Hinami had picked up a largish tin button.

"Oh, okay."

"It's so summery. I love it!" She smiled sweetly.

I followed her gaze to the button she wanted. It was a nice picture of colorful fireworks against a black background. I was surprised she went for it, though. Sure, it was bright and pretty, but...what did she like so much about it?

She picked it up daintily.

"You like that stuff?" I asked bluntly.

Hinami seemed briefly unsure. "I wouldn't normally buy stuff without a reason, but...this just struck me."

I made a noncommittal sound in response to this uncharacteristic vagueness. So even she wanted things sometimes without a good reason. Or was this all part of the act?

I looked over the other pins for sale. There were Japanese flags; popular anime characters; rice balls, fried eggs, and other kinds of food; animals like frogs and scorpions—you name it. Basically, there were tons of choices, all for only a couple hundred yen or so. From among all this, she wanted that bright one with fireworks on it? I didn't get it.

In the passageway, a guy and girl who seemed to be on a date were looking at stuff together. They made me feel self-conscious about heroine-mode Hinami's girlish behavior. *W-we're not on a date, okay?! This is just a dress rehearsal!*

"So this is what you want to trade for?"

I was getting a little worked up, almost shy, even though there was really nothing going on between us. Hiding it as best I could, I took the pin from Hinami.

"Yeah! Is that all right with you?"

I looked at the price tag. It was four hundred yen plus tax. Not good.

"It's…uh…I mean, I feel like it's not fair for me to be getting that bag for just four hundred yen…"

"Sheesh! I said I want it; that should be enough!" She playfully grabbed my arm with both hands and pressed it against my chest, pin and all. Then she pushed me from behind and steered me over to the register.

"O-okay, okay."

"Thank you!"

Her pushy, almost businesslike behavior made me wonder. Sure, maybe she really did want that pin, but it was more likely that she was creating a "fair trade" just to erase my guilt over getting something for free. Then I could take the backpack without reservations and not feel indebted to her in the future. And if that was the case, then—wow. She wasn't being self-serving or pushy. That was genuine thoughtfulness.

Maybe this ability to consider other people's feelings was the key factor that kept her at the top of our high school's cast of characters as the perfect heroine. At least, that was the vague sense I had.

I let her push me to the register, where I paid for the pin and…would it be right to say I gave it to Hinami as a present? No, this was a trade. Anyway, that was how I ended up trading Hinami a fireworks pin for her black backpack.

"Um, thanks."

"No worries. I'm going to take good care of it!" she chirped before tucking the pin into her bag with a gentle, happy smile. It hit me right in the feels. Man, she was a good actress.

* * *

I was standing in front of an *Atafami* game console. Our two ninja characters were on the screen.

Hinami and I were at the console in Big Camera, where I'd led us, playing for the first to win three games with a stock of three. I'd already won two games, which meant it would be a shutout for me if I won this game. Hinami and I both had one stock left.

Heroine mode had vanished. She was pure NO NAME now, her determination on full display.

"It's not over yet…!" she muttered fervently as she performed a close-edge recovery. Even though she was worked up, the move was extremely well planned, and even I failed at blocking her.

"Nice…!!"

I was secretly surprised. Both Hinami and I were playing with the ninja character Found. As usual, her playstyle was to copy and defend against my own. Nothing had changed, except for one thing.

Hinami was improving way faster than I expected.

Each move was precise, she knew how to play the mental game, and every risk was well calculated. She had a wide variety of offensive patterns at her disposal and flexible defensive patterns. On top of that, her already superhuman ability to escape combos had somehow gotten even better. I couldn't believe she'd improved this much in the space of the mere week or two we hadn't played while everything was happening with Mimimi.

From mid-distance, Hinami pretended she was about to launch a projectile, canceled into a block, then canceled again into a wavedash that took her skimming along the ground. From there, she dashed at me. Her ulterior motive was probably to use the projectile to lure me into blocking, which would give her enough time to reach me with her insane technique and punch me at close range.

"…Ha-ha."

I couldn't help laughing.

I've played a lot of people in my day; I know that some of them figured if they put in X amount more effort, they could get within range of beating me, and that spurred them to work harder. But even after putting in the work, they'd never been able to beat me. That was because I'd been working harder than them in the meantime and gained more ground. I was starting out in first, and I improved faster than anyone else—that's how I kept my position as the best player in Japan. And that hadn't changed. But Hinami—Hinami was different.

For these past few weeks, probably the past couple of months or so, maybe even since she started playing, she'd been improving at a slightly faster rate than me.

That was why I had to laugh. It had never happened to me before, and it made me weirdly happy. It was exciting to know someone else out there loved *Atafami* as much as I did and was working just as hard. I wasn't alone. When that thought hit me all over again, I couldn't help smiling.

Just playing her made it obvious what she'd been doing with her time lately.

For Hinami and me, *Atafami* was the ideal form of communication. That's exactly why I was determined not to let up—why I *couldn't* let up.

Aiming to neutralize her strategy, I wavedashed out of my block—but I didn't slide across the ground. In other words, I did a wavedash out of shield to take advantage of the invincibility frames, and from there, in a single flowing movement, I entered the command for my Attack. My Found character wrapped his right arm around his own neck. Hinami's character ran toward him. *Come and get it.*

This Attack is where the name *Attack Families* comes from. It's a special blow that can damage your opponent in proportion to the amount of start-up lag or ending lag in their Attack, thus increasing the knockback. It can be a game-winning counter to use when your opponent is seriously unguarded, but that's not all. Charging it up and timing it to finish off a combo is also one of Found's distinctive moves. I used that to intercept Hinami's blow.

But I had miscalculated.

I'm not sure if she'd seen me charging the Attack or whether it was pure instinct. In this case, her reaction was so instantaneous it seemed more realistic to attribute it to nonrational instinct than to superhuman reflexes.

Either way, Hinami switched her path of action.

She canceled her blow, blocked my Attack at super-close range, and landed a blow during my Attack's ending animation. Then she moved into a decisive combo, the ideal, stable strategy that gave her an overwhelming advantage.

...I lied. That's not what she did.

Instead, she canceled her dash with a wavedash and wrapped her right arm around her neck. She was trying to launch an Attack head-on without charging before I had a chance to launch mine after charging. It was a crazy, ambitious, extremely confident move.

"...Shit!"

I realized what she was up to a second before it was too late and released my Attack. My backhanded blow crossed paths with Hinami's. And then...

"Yeah! Bam!"

"Damn!!"

My blow crashed into Hinami an instant before hers reached me. Her Found character soared off the stage.

In the end, I won the game with two stocks left, and the three-game match ended in a straight-set win for me.

* * *

Hinami and I were in Starbucks.

"I-if I tap here..."

"She gets added to your contact list!"

"Uh, and a notification gets sent right away..."

"What? Of course! Obviously."

"O-oh, okay..."

I was facing the screen to add Fuka Kikuchi as a friend on LINE, locked in an internal struggle. Hinami was back in heroine mode, but ever since losing at *Atafami*, she'd been slightly grumpy.

As soon as I sat down at Starbucks, my phone had vibrated with a message from her containing Kikuchi-san's LINE ID. All I had to do was touch the ADD button. Impressive technology. Still, several minutes had passed by without me doing anything.

"But if I add her out of the blue, won't she be confused?"

I mean, if I added her, she'd all of a sudden get a message saying, [*Fumiya Tomozaki added you as a friend*], right? This was me we were talking about; the thought made my stomach turn.

"The heck are you talking about? That's not an issue." Hinami grinned.

"Huh?"

She was talking a little more roughly than usual, and I wasn't sure what she meant.

"I mean, I already told her you wanted to add her on LINE and asked if it would be okay!"

"Hey...!" I caught myself just before my voice rose above a Starbucks-appropriate volume.

"Wow, Tomozaki. You've learned how to keep your voice down when you're surprised. You're really improving."

"Th-that's not the kind of improvement I need..."

The tiny hit of sarcasm from heroine-mode Hinami stung ten times more than usual.

"The point is, you've got some nerve asking her without my permission..."

"But it would have been wrong to give you her ID without asking first, so I would have had to ask her anyway...and I thought it would be better to just go ahead and do it..." Heroine Hinami cast her eyes down sadly. I almost apologized for making her sad, but the little quirk of her lips gave her away. She just wanted to mess with me. *I'm not* that *gullible, Hinami.*

Anyway, she'd already talked to Kikuchi-san.

"What did Kikuchi-san say?" I asked, tensing up.

"Huh? She said it was fine, obviously!" Hinami tilted her head adorably.

"R-really...?" Her simple blow took the wind out of my sails. "Okay, then."

I nodded, as if at her command. It was so frustrating. But adding someone as a friend wasn't such a big deal, right? I'd asked Mimimi if I could add her myself; compared to that, this should be a sure bet. I fired myself up and held my breath.

"...There!"

I boldly tapped the ADD button. I'd done it.

"Nicely done. It would have been even better if you asked her directly, but...you didn't really have a chance, right?"

"Uh, yeah."

I nodded, my face flushing from her compliment. *Please just stop, Hinami.*

But at least I'd accomplished one task. I let out a long breath and took my first sip of the iced latte I'd ordered.

"...Hey, Tomozaki-kun? You haven't sent her a message yet, have you? What was that sigh of relief for?"

"Oh."

Another hit from heroine Hinami. She was right, though. I was way too satisfied with myself just for adding Kikuchi-san as a friend. I was already acting like I'd reached some kind of goal, but the truth was, today's goal was to ask her out.

"I think all you'll need to do today is send her a short message."

"Yeah? What if she writes back?"

"Well, with someone like Yuzu, if you send a LINE message she'll fire back immediately, but with someone like Fuka-chan, even if she reads it right away, you won't get a reply for a long time. Her type tends to treat LINE like e-mail and letters!"

"Yeah...that does sound like Kikuchi-san."

Most kids like us would fire off messages constantly, but she would take her time and respond at a leisurely pace, like correspondence on paper. That sounded about right for the fairy of the library. I could totally see it.

"I'll leave the content up to you. I think you'll be fine as long as you mention I gave you her ID and that you want to see a movie over summer vacation!"

"What? You're leaving it up to me...?"

Reeling a little, I remembered she had told me before that it was time for me to train my ability to think for myself now that I'd learned to take action.

"S-so...thinking about the content is part of my training right now?"

"Hexactly," she said with a grin. Guess she used that word even in heroine mode.

I had no idea where to start with the message.

"...This is tough."

Still, all I could do was give it my best. *Here goes, then.* All in the name of training.

I nodded stiffly and quietly began typing. Glancing up between thoughts, I caught sight of Hinami dreamily sucking up a sherbet-like orange liquid from her cup. She was lost in her own world. She only looked that happy when she was eating, even if it wasn't cheese. Honestly, at moments like these, she was incredibly cute.

As I was gazing helplessly at her strangely girlish, innocent expression, she looked over at me. Her eyes were sharp as they met mine.

"…What?"

"…Nothing."

Hinami suddenly and threateningly snapped out of heroine mode and into real Hinami with such force it gave me whiplash. I conceded complete defeat and returned to my message. I'd been briefly charmed by her expression, but I was wrong. She wasn't cute.

Anyway, um…for the moment, I figured I'd focus on not writing something weird. Yeah, that was the way to go. After all, that was about all I was capable of. *Man.* Everyone acts like LINE is so easy, but I sure was having a hard time.

After a few minutes, I looked up.

"Whew. Done."

When I completed the message, I noticed that Hinami had finished her orange liquid. *Don't you think you should slow down with the sweet drinks?*

"Ooh…show me, show me!"

I passed my phone to Hinami, who had returned to heroine mode like she'd never left it. This was the message typed on the screen:

[*Hinami gave me your LINE ID.*

I read another Andi book since last time we talked. This one was really good, too.

So how about the idea I mentioned before of going to see the movie based on his book in Shibuya?

Let me know when you're free!]

Hinami stared at the message with concern. *Wh-what?! What's that look for?*

"Wh-what do you think…?" I asked anxiously.

Hinami looked at me, her expression unchanged. "Well, maybe the awkwardness is for the best…"

"Um, wh-what do you mean…?" I asked quietly. That comment only made me more worried.

"I think…it's fine if you send it like this."

Hinami sounded unusually unsure of herself, and suddenly everything was weird. Was this because she was in heroine mode? Or was my message so questionable it even undermined Hinami's confidence?

"Uh, um, so…?"

"Yeah…let's send this…okay?" She tilted her head to the side. Guess that was a green light?

"Okay…" I channeled energy into my finger. "Send!"

I summoned all my courage and hit the SEND button. Then I asked Hinami to make sure I'd actually sent it.

"Yup. Now all you have to do is wait for a response. I think it should come sometime today!"

"Oh, okay."

"Well, good job. That should be enough for today. Get in touch with me when you hear from Kikuchi-san, all right? Actually, never mind—you might as well think about what to say back yourself. I'll leave it to you! I'll let you know when I have more information about the overnight trip."

"O-okay."

"As for your last assignment…"

"Huh?" Just when I thought I was done, here comes another assignment. *Shocker.*

"I said there might be another assignment after the date, didn't I?"

"Da…"

This wasn't a date; it was special training! But when she said that word in heroine mode, it hit home all the same. Yet even as her wicked smile delivered the sucker punch, I remembered what she'd said.

"Oh yeah. You said you might have another one for me, depending on how things were going."

"Right. I've been thinking…"

Hinami stared down at the receipt from our drinks. "Lately, you've been buying clothes and eating out, and if you come camping with us, you'll have to pay for that, too."

"...Yeah." I *was* a little worried about that.

"So I was thinking that pretty soon your savings might run dry."

Recalling the contents of my wallet earlier, I replied solemnly, "To tell you the truth, you're right."

Hinami sighed and nodded. "Thought so. You'd better start soon, then."

"Start what?"

She frowned in exasperation. "A part-time job? Obviously!"

"A job...?"

My summer was already looking Spartan enough with the assignments from school and today, but to add a job to that...?

Hinami was fiddling with her phone. "If you have just one insular relationship, you're not actually seeing the full picture, and other things may seem arbitrary and unpredictable even though they make perfect sense. So not only will you earn some cash, but this will be a chance to learn from a new perspective!"

"Oh, uh-huh... Yeah, I think this was inevitable..."

That was definitely true in terms of money. If I was going to be buying a bunch of new clothes and going out to do stuff I didn't usually do, my regular allowance wasn't going to cut it. My parents assumed I didn't have any friends, so aside from my New Year's money, they kept my allowance to a bare minimum. They sure do know their kid.

"That's why I want you to interview for some jobs around here!" Hinami showed me her phone. At the same moment, my own phone vibrated.

"Huh?"

Even though I had a few more friends than I used to, I still hardly ever got texts or calls. I jumped a little in surprise and checked the screen.

"...Um, Hinami?" I felt like my brain had reached capacity. Everything went blank.

"Yes?" she answered sweetly. *Come on, stop messing with me! Wait, that's not the issue right now.*

"Y-you said it would take her a while to write back..."

"...Huh?" She looked at my phone.

There was a LINE message from Kikuchi-san. Hinami tapped the screen expressionlessly.

"Hey!" I said as we read the message together.

[*I'd love to go!*
I can make time any day other than Tuesdays and Wednesdays in August!
What is your schedule like?]

Hinami was mildly surprised at the message, which had taken less than ten minutes to arrive. Then she rested her chin on her palm as if she was plotting something, raised her eyebrows teasingly, and gave me one of her sadistic smiles.

"Sounds like she's really looking forward to seeing that movie with you."

"Wha...?"

With that, my brain circuits fizzled, my face turned hot, and I couldn't say another word.

That was the end of our first date—I mean, the first special training day of summer.

Later, after I had cooled down enough to listen to Hinami's advice, Kikuchi-san and I exchanged some more extremely polite e-mails and managed to arrange a movie date. Monday, August 1. Four days away.

I felt like I was going to explode if I had to think about one more thing.

Honestly, though...I was a little happy, too. After all, even if we're just friends who both like Andi's novels, she still agreed to go see a movie with just me. And if that was the case, I had a responsibility to do everything I could to prepare.

I figured I'd spend the next day memorizing conversation topics, practicing my tone, doing image training, and generally getting ready for our date. But that's not how it all went down, because this summer vacation Hinami-san was in charge.

* * *

It was the following night, and I was getting ready to go to sleep.

I lay in bed flipping through flash cards with conversation topics on them, unusually tense because the movie date was only three days away.

[*Don't make any plans on August fourth or fifth.*]

Hinami's LINE message got right to the point, and it would be the first of several about the overnight trip. I put the flash cards down next to my pillow and picked up my phone.

[*What's up?*]

[*Yuzu, Mimimi, Nakamura, Mizusawa, Takei, and I are having a BBQ, and you can come.*]

[*Wait a second*]

She had suddenly decided to share her big secret, I see. I guess it makes her happy to push my limits. Yeah, it definitely does.

[*We're going to spend the night*
Are you free?]

[*Yeah, but just wait a second*]

[*We're going to meet at Mimimi's house to plan everything.*
Are you free tomorrow or the next day?]

[*Can you slow down?!*] Once again, my brain circuits were about to fry as I aggressively swiped my reply into the phone.

[*Yes or no?*]

[*I'm free both days*]

[*Thought so.*]

[*What's that supposed to mean?*]

I do get why she would say that, of course.

[*Anyway, we're meeting tomorrow afternoon at Kitayono Station.*
I'll let you know when we decide on an exact time.]

[*Hey, what's this BBQ gonna be like? When? Where? Is this the overnight you were talking about?*]

The notification popped up showing she'd read my message, and a beat later, my phone started playing music.

La-la-la...

Out of surprise at this unusual occurrence, I dropped my phone on the bed, which made the chaos several times worse. When I gingerly picked it up and looked at the screen, I saw that Hinami was calling me through the app. *Huh? You can make phone calls on LINE?*

With timid, shaking fingers, I swiped the button to answer the call.

"Hel…hello?"

"Can you hear me?"

That strangely beautiful, clear, confident voice reached my ear.

"Yeah, I can hear you…but why did you call me?"

"Huh? 'Cause it was going to be annoying to write a text."

"Oh right."

I guess talking on the phone was no big deal for normies. I, on the other hand, got nervous just hearing the word *phone*. I don't trust myself to carry a conversation.

"Anyway, the basic story with the overnight is we're trying to get Yuzu and Nakamura together."

Since I couldn't see her body language, I was extra focused on her voice. I should be used to it by now, but I felt like that clear, melodic sound was penetrating straight into my brain.

"Huh."

For some reason, I was sitting on my bed with my legs folded under me like a proper disciple as we talked. Of course, this was the first time I was talking on the phone with someone my age of the opposite sex, so it felt kind of like a secret conversation. The fact that we were talking right before bed shook me up, too, so I hardly registered what she was saying.

"Recently, you've been able to have normal conversations with Yuzu and Mimimi and Hanabi and Fuka-chan, but you still don't have many guy friends, and that's a big issue."

"Oh yeah… That's true."

I tried to absorb what Hinami was saying despite my pounding heart. The thing about not having guy friends had occurred to me before.

"On the trip, you'll develop your male friendships. Plus, spending two days surrounded by normies will gain you major EXP. Those are your goals."

The breeze from the air conditioner further chilled the cold sweat dripping down my neck.

"So what were you saying about getting Nakamura and Yuzu together?"

"That's the main goal of the trip. They refuse to just go out, so the idea started with the other five of us. We wanted to make it happen."

"Ha-ha-ha... What a normie plan..."

I was still sitting perfectly still with my legs folded under me, my back straight.

"Since that's the point of the trip, I'm hoping you won't interfere, and if there's something you can do to help, I'd like you to do it. But I doubt there's much you can do, and it's hard to focus on two separate goals, so you shouldn't worry about it too much."

"I see..."

Socializing with Nakamura, Mizusawa, and Takei and trying to make male friends was a fairly heavy load for me already. If I had to strategize ways to bring Nakamura and Izumi together on top of that, I'd be severely overworked.

Anyway, now I knew the goal here. I'd been right there with Izumi as she earnestly tried to choose a present that Nakamura would like, so I did honestly hope it would work out between them. Plus, I *am* Izumi's mentor after all.

"It shouldn't cost more than ten thousand yen... Do you have that much?"

"T-ten thousand..." I thought about my bank balance. "Maybe...just barely."

"Well, worst-case scenario I can lend you some cash, but if it's really gonna be tough for you, you don't have to come, okay? As far as money goes, I mean."

"Um..."

My quickly frying brain waffled for a minute. It *was* going to be tight. On the other hand, I could imagine how hard she'd worked to get me accepted into the group. I'd be starting a part-time job soon, and this would be a big training opportunity...

My fingers tightened around the phone. "No, I'll go," I said very clearly and decisively.

"...Okay. In that case, meet us tomorrow at Kitayono Station like I said. Probably around two. We'll be talking about the Yuzu-Nakamura strategy, so it'll just be Mimimi and Mizusawa and me."

"Oh, okay."

Based on who was coming, tomorrow's meeting wouldn't be too hard for me.

"Takei is coming on the trip, but he's generally useless and would probably just get in the way; he's not coming to the meeting. He doesn't even know what the trip is for."

"Oh..." Wow, way to dunk on the guy.

"As far as your assignment for tomorrow's meeting goes..."

"Yeah?"

So she had an assignment in mind. Figures.

"I want you to mess with Mizusawa three times tomorrow."

"M-mess with him?"

That sounded kind of aggressive; now I was getting nervous.

"Yes. It's fine to just argue with something he says. Do you know why I want you to do this?"

"No...," I answered honestly, and Hinami launched into a brisk explanation.

"There's a very common problem non-normies make when they want to change their social status and that is to go along with whatever the normies say."

"Go along with whatever they say?"

"Yes," Hinami said in her quiet, beautiful voice. I felt like the speaker in my phone was sighing. "When a non-normie tries to join a normie group, they often agree with whatever the in-group says and act like they're happy about everything in a desperate attempt to belong."

"...Yeah, I can see that."

Makes sense when you think about it. If you don't know how to become friends, you probably start by trying to demonstrate that you're just like them. But I had some doubts.

"Are you saying that's wrong?"

It was an honest question. I mean, if you could become friends just by agreeing with someone, that would be a great way of becoming a normie.

"Yes, it's a huge mistake. The best position you'll ever gain through that strategy is as a designated punching bag. You may be temporarily accepted, but you'll never be an equal. You're just a poser."

"A poser…"

I'd seen that word online a bunch of times. I think it meant a normie who was always changing based on what seemed trendy or cool.

"Posers are those stupid people who base their whole identity on belonging to the popular group. They don't have any friends who treat them as equals, and everything they do is defined by their attempts to fit the values of the group they want to be a part of. In that sense they're even worse than loners, so you should definitely avoid intentionally going in that direction. Basically, you just need to remember the end goal we set right at the beginning, which is for you to become a normie on the same level as me."

I couldn't help smiling cynically at Hinami as she delivered this cut-and-dried explanation.

"I get it—don't become a poser, because then I'll never be an equal. But you're saying the assignment that will help me do that is to mess with Mizusawa three times?"

I lowered my voice so my parents and sister wouldn't hear our conversation. They sure would be surprised if they heard me talking about posers and equal friendships. I was still sitting on my knees.

"Yes. It's a way to build a friendship where you're at least an equal. Instead of agreeing with the person all the time, you mess with them a little, make some pointed comments, challenge them when you disagree with them. That way, it's harder for them to treat you like an idiot or mess with you."

"…Makes sense."

Something occurred to me at that point. What she was saying sounded similar to what I called the Mizusawa Method, where you said something harsh but it somehow didn't mess up the relationship. Huh. So the effect of that was to create a relationship where you were at least equal to the other person. Pretty amazing that Mizusawa did that naturally.

"Simply put, the high school hierarchy is ultimately based on whether a person is able to mess with lots of other people or not."

"…Oh."

I understood her point intuitively. Now that she'd laid it out for me, I could see that the reason Nakamura was among the most powerful people in our class was that no one could mess with him, but he could mess with whomever he wanted. I mean, Nakamura wouldn't be Nakamura if he didn't give people crap, and I also couldn't imagine him being the butt of everyone else's jokes… You know, in that light, human relationships start to seem kinda scary.

"Of course, if you do it too much, people will see you as overly aggressive or annoying, and your position will fall. That's why I've put a limit on your assignment."

"Oh, gotcha."

The fact that she'd said "three times" instead of "at least three times" was apparently important.

"Anyway, that's your assignment. You should be careful not to tease him about anything too weird, but he basically thinks you're interesting because of the way you told Erika Konno off, so I think he'll let a mistake or two slide. That's why I chose him for this assignment."

"Wow, you sure did think this through…"

"Obviously."

I could imagine her usual triumphant expression.

"That's about it. Do you understand the general idea? Any questions?"

"N-no, I'm fine. I got it."

"Really? Okay, then I'll see you tomorrow."

"Right, see you then."

Suddenly the line went dead. I was left alone, legs still folded under me, with the quiet hum of the air conditioner filling the cool room. I realized how nervous I'd been through the whole conversation.

So tomorrow. I had more vacation homework ahead of me. The assignment was to mess with the super-normie Mizusawa three times…? Could I pull it off?

"Well, for now…"

I pulled open my desk drawer and put away the flash cards I'd prepared for Kikuchi-san. Tomorrow's meeting would consist of Hinami, Mimimi, and Mizusawa.

"In which case…this and this should work."

I pulled out two new stacks of conversation cards and flipped through them. I figured that if I was going to push back against someone in the group, I'd have to make sure my base of memorized topics was especially solid. If it wasn't, my brain wouldn't be able to both participate in the group conversation and think about my assignment. I knew that the more I memorized, the more smoothly my conversations would go and the easier it would be for me to interact with other people, and I got a little zing of accomplishment every time I memorized a new topic. It was actually getting to be fun. I guess when you see the results of your efforts, making that effort stops feeling like such a burden.

I'd memorized the bulk of the topics when I realized there was something else I had to do. Might as well ride the wave and do it right now. I took out my phone, went to the website Hinami had sent me before, and tapped the phone number. It rang a few times before someone picked up.

"Thank you for your calling the Karaoke Sevens Omiya facility. How can I help you?"

"Um…I'm calling about your job notice online…"

Within a few minutes, I'd set up an interview for August 3, five days from now.

That meant tomorrow, July 30, I'd go to the strategy meeting at Mimimi's house. On August 1, I'd go see a movie with Kikuchi-san. On the third, I'd have an interview for a summer job. Then on the fourth and fifth, I'd go on the overnight barbecue trip.

This really was shaping up to be a summer vacation with no rest, but maybe it wouldn't be so bad after all.

* * *

The next day was July 30, the day of the meeting.

Just as Hinami had predicted, we were supposed to meet at Kitayono Station at two. I arrived at the station about five minutes early and stood there roasting in the blazing sun. I was wearing the pants and shoes from the mannequin outfit and the T-shirt Hinami had chosen for me two days earlier.

Apparently, the plan was for the four of us to meet up and go to Mimimi's house to talk. I'd been to a girl's room twice before—once when Hinami dragged me to her place and once when I went to Izumi's house to teach her *Atafami*—but both of those times were unusual situations. The experience was still totally new for me, and I couldn't help feeling nervous.

Looking around to see if anyone else was there yet, I spotted Mizusawa leaning against a shady wall, looking at his phone. Everything about him was pure *cool.* He was just standing there, though; why was I feeling that way? Based on what Hinami had taught me, I guessed it was the overall impression created from his clothes, hair, posture, expression—all the little details. Mizusawa naturally scored incredibly high in all those areas. My stomach hurt just thinking about the fact that I had to mess with or challenge this super normie three times today.

I gave myself a little pep talk, approached him, and made eye contact when he noticed me.

"Hey, Fumiya."

"H-hey."

With an agreeable, breezy smile, he dropped the polite suffix from my name and raised a hand in greeting. It was a simple combination of words and action, but it demonstrated a powerful coolness I could never achieve. These little behaviors added up gradually to determine whether it was okay to push them around a little. I already felt on the verge of giving up. But I had to at least try.

Mess with him or challenge him. Three times.

Mizusawa wiped the sweat from his cheeks with his hand. "Damn, it's hot today."

It crossed my mind to argue with him right then and there—*Really, you think it's hot? I disagree*—but since it was undeniably hot, I decided to agree with him. Close call. I was about to become that weird guy.

"Y-yeah."

I thought I'd reached the point where I could say "Yeah" without stuttering, but since I was thinking about how to contradict him at the same time, it didn't come out so smooth.

"Hope this trip goes well," Mizusawa said, giggling like a happy kid. His smile was friendly. His usual coolness was still there, but there was a softness along with it. Maybe this was one of those smiles that inspires the maternal instinct...

Anyway, even I knew that it would be weird to argue back on that point (*It's not necessarily for the best if it goes well, in my opinion. Other guys might like Izumi, too, you know?*), so once again I let the conversation flow along smoothly. Aside from my current assignment, I still had to do the basic work of developing a topic, right? *Uh, we're talking about the trip... Yeah, I had something memorized for that.*

"You mean the strategy to get Izumi and Nakamura together?" Pulling up an appropriate comment from my stock, I delivered it in a slightly joking tone.

"Yeah!"

"Uh, for two people who like each other, they sure are taking forever to get together."

I made a conscious effort to advance the discussion myself. I'd recorded and practiced the nonchalant delivery multiple times, so I don't think I sounded weird. Still, it felt harder than usual because I also had to look for opportunities to push him.

"Before we launched this plan, I did ask Yuzu when the hell they were going to start dating."

"Oh yeah?"

"She said she wants to date him, but she can't make the first move... She's too chicken."

"Er, ha-ha, yeah, Izumi isn't very brave when it comes to stuff like that."

I smiled as I tried to sound like a normie. I must have been thinking too much about how to mess with Mizusawa, because I ended up ragging on someone who wasn't even there instead. Pretty sure Hinami wouldn't count that.

"Those two'll talk your ear off, but when it comes to this stuff, they're super naive. Those two idiots are making us do all the work."

He smiled amiably again. While I was tripping over myself to find something only slightly rude to say, with questionable results, he'd just showed me how it was done with that light, smooth, agreeable, totally harsh comment. His harshness was directed at people who weren't here, just like mine was, but damn he was good. I felt like I was observing a textbook example.

"So it's not just Izumi, huh? I'm surprised Nakamura is like that, too."

I thought back to when Izumi gave Nakamura the present. His reaction made me think he was fairly interested. Even I had seen some hope there.

Mizusawa lowered his voice comically. "Basically, he's a simple guy. I mean, just look at the way he gets all excited about *Atafami*."

"True."

I nodded, matching my mood to Mizusawa's casual one. I managed to brush away the revoltingly weak question that kept crossing my mind about whether I was even allowed to talk on such equal terms with Mizusawa. I had to think of him as an equal...but no, it was impossible to see myself on equal terms with someone so cool.

"Of course, you can't talk when it comes to *Atafami*, can you? You're an idiot yourself on that front."

"Ah-ha-ha...you're right there."

With that, Mizusawa managed to needle me before I'd messed with him. And to top it off, I didn't even mind that much. Total failure.

"I dunno if he even knows how to set himself up for anything. I'm not sure if I'd call him honest or just plain stupid."

His smile was both exasperated and vaguely amused. *Amazing.* This whole time he's naturally and effortlessly doing what I'm struggling so hard to achieve. I smiled along, but at the same time, I was searching for my opportunity to get in a jab. Just then, Mimimi and Hinami showed up. *Shit. I'm at zero points so far.*

"Hey! You guys sure are early!!"

Mimimi walked toward us, swinging her arms energetically. She was wearing a T-shirt and jeans, which even I could see was a really simple outfit, but she was naturally attractive enough that it still grabbed your attention.

"Sorry to make you wait!"

Hinami was wearing some white thing with fluffy sleeves and a grayish skirt. A bag with a pale-yellow strap was slung over her shoulder. I'd never seen the bag before. Then I noticed she was also wearing a big blue watch—also new to me—and she had some sort of sparkly jewel on her left ear. Which made me think she'd been very careful in choosing her outfit. I'm not one to say, but it looked perfect to me.

"Long time no see, huh?! Heya, Brain!" Mimimi thumped my shoulder with her signature excessive force. It hurt, but I was glad to see her back to her energetic old self.

Mizusawa was looking at us suspiciously. "Brain? Oh yeah, I kind of remember you mentioned that before in the dining hall."

"Yup!" Mimimi said, giving him a thumbs-up. I thought back to the time we'd run into the Nakamura Faction during one of our student council strategy meetings in the cafeteria. We'd told him that I was the "brain" of her campaign and I was helping write her speech.

"Oh, um, yeah... Ha-ha-ha."

I laughed, hoping he wouldn't figure out that the stunt we pulled during the speech was all choreographed. Mizusawa's face went blank for a second, but then he glanced around at the group and continued talking. "So should we get going? We're going to Mimimi's place, right? Which way is it?"

"Oh, sorry, guys...," Mimimi said, pressing her hands together in front of her face like she was praying for our forgiveness. "My grandma ended up coming over today. Can we go to a diner or something instead?" She winked and looked at each of us in turn.

"Sure, no worries. I think there's a Saizeriya around here and a Jonathan's, too, right?"

"Oh, oops!" Mimimi squealed, like she'd just realized something.

"What's wrong?" Mizusawa asked.

"I just remembered," she said, looking at me for some reason. "Your house is near Kitayono, too, isn't it, Tomozaki?"

"Huh?" This was unexpected; I wasn't sure how to react. "Yeah, it is, but..."

"Then why don't we go there?!" She brought her palms together again, this time pleading.

"Uh, um…"

As I was fumbling for words, Hinami piled on. "Oh, good idea! Would that be okay, Tomozaki?"

Damn. That was her order for me to go along with it. I had no idea whether this was part of my special training or merely her sadistic side coming out, but I had no other choice.

"Um…no, it's not a problem."

"Yay, Tomozaki! Comin' in clutch!"

"Fumiya's house, huh? Looking forward to that," Mizusawa added.

Mimimi strode forward, taking the lead. "Okay, let's get going!" But she was going in the opposite direction from my house.

"Um, that's the wrong way. It's the same direction as your house, I think."

"Oh yeah, right!"

Mimimi turned back toward me, laughing off her mistake, then strode off again. She was hopeless. I followed somewhat timidly.

"Let's search his house."

"Definitely!"

Behind me, Mizusawa and Hinami were teasing me. Damn, I was getting messed with nonstop, and I hadn't managed one little jab. Guess that's the fate of bottom-tier characters.

* * *

"H-Hinami-senpai…and Nanami-senpai…and Mizusawa-senpai…?!"

My little sister had come down to the door when we got there, and she was staring at us with both hands over her mouth and nose as if she were witnessing a natural disaster.

"Um, mind if we use the house for a while? I promise we won't leave my room…"

"N-no problem! And no worries, you can leave your room!"

She gazed at the three older kids with sparkling, excited eyes. What was with her? No, I could see what was going on. Here I was with the perfect heroine of our school, Aoi Hinami, along with the cool, studly guy who had given a speech introducing her during the student council elections, and the number-two member of the track team who had challenged Hinami's gold-star team in the election.

The three of them were probably the most famous second-year students at Sekitomo High School right now.

Given my sister's fangirling, she apparently was very excited to see these three idols together in person. Plus me, from the bottom of the hierarchy, which had thrown her entire worldview for a loop.

"Mom! Tomozaki brought some friends… Friends? Er, some cool kids from his class over to our house!!"

"What?! Fumiya…brought kids from his class over?! Friends?! What is going on?!"

"I don't know! It's weird, right?!"

"What should we do?! Should I go buy a cake or something?!"

"I don't know! Maybe some red rice and beans?!"

"Should I start cooking some?!"

"Oh, shut up, you two! Leave me alone!"

Mimimi started laughing as my family descended into chaos.

"…What?"

"Nothing! Your family's just funny!"

"I feel like that wasn't a compliment…"

At that point, Mizusawa started laughing, too. "Nah, I think it was, dude!"

"What? Really…?" Right then, I remembered my assignment. "No, I'm pretty sure it wasn't."

"Ha-ha-ha! Really?"

"Uh, yeah."

I'd managed to muster a minor revolt against Mizusawa. Would this count as one time? It was a very tiny contradiction. On the other hand, if I hadn't had that assignment, I never would have said it. And now that I had, I felt I'd expressed my own thoughts in a small way. I was starting to see how doing this over and over could lead to an equal relationship.

As all these thoughts ran through my head, I took off my shoes so I could bring everyone up to my room. After Mimimi and Mizusawa took theirs off, they both grinned and looked back and forth between me and the living room, where my mom and sister were standing. I glanced back at Hinami

to see if she'd noticed my comment to Mizusawa. She was briskly lining everyone's shoes up in a neat row in the entryway. Then she stood up like she hadn't done anything special and walked over to me.

"...What?" she asked.

"Oh, nothing..."

She was amazing in so many ways.

We all headed up to my room.

"Ooh, Brain, I see something sketchy!"

With that, Mimimi, Mizusawa, and Hinami began a thorough inspection of my private space. There was my bed and my desk, a little CRT TV I used for playing old games, and a console for playing *Atafami*. Aside from that and a small laptop laying on my bed, there wasn't much in my drab Western-style bedroom. *Search all you want, guys. You won't find anything!*

"What is this?! There are so many controllers in here!" Mimimi said excitedly as she pulled a plastic bag out of my desk. It was full of controllers that I'd burned through and planned to get rid of later.

"Oh, those are just practice controllers for *Atafami*. They aren't good anymore..."

"You went through this many?!"

"Yeah, you use that many over two or three years. I can't bring myself to get rid of them because they're still good for other games..."

The joysticks weren't too worn down for regular use, so it didn't seem right to throw them out. They just wouldn't work in *Atafami* because it required such delicate joystick maneuvers.

"Huh...you really are intense when it comes to stuff like that," Mimimi said, returning the bag gently to its drawer.

"Yeah, I guess I am."

Mizusawa burst out laughing at my fairly confident answer.

"What?"

"Nothing... It's just—you really are a weirdo."

I didn't get it. *Wait...is he messing with me again?* "What's so weird about it?"

I pushed back, hoping I might get another point out of this.

"It's just funny, dude," he said, cackling. "Right, Ao—"

He glanced back at Hinami and stopped midsentence. Thinking that was odd, I followed his glance and saw that Hinami was reaching into the plastic bag of controllers and touching each one with her finger to see how worn down the joysticks were.

"Aoi?"

She flinched a little when Mizusawa called her name, which wasn't like her. Gradually, the look in her eyes transitioned from total seriousness back to perfect heroine.

"It's such a waste to throw these away... If I were your mom, I'd be so upset...!"

"Ha-ha-ha! What are you talking about? I didn't know you were such a penny-pincher!"

"But it's a waste...! I am *appalled*!"

She ad-libbed along with Mizusawa, playing a silly character. She was truly amazing.

"Seriously, though," Mizusawa said, sitting down next to Hinami. "This is real commitment."

He peered into Hinami's face. Was he talking about my commitment to *Atafami*? More importantly, they were sitting *waaay* too close to each other. A genuine in-your-face conversation between a handsome guy and a beautiful girl.

"...Huh? Did I say that?"

Hinami looked him in the eye, apparently unwilling to go along with him. What was she doing? True, she'd been talking about wasting resources, not commitment. Still, she was so close to him with those glistening eyes. Guess this was a normie tactic? I was impressed. A battle between two strong characters.

"What? I totally assumed that's what you were thinking. It's incredible. Shows how serious he is."

Mizusawa grinned. Even as a guy, I knew he was attractive, and he was smiling at her at close range. A cross counterattack involving a smile and upturned eyes. Would it manage to inflict damage on Hinami? Also, for some reason his tone was ironic, but I'm not sure why.

"You could be right."

Hinami grinned, too. No visible damage. A draw, then.

"...Anyway, let's get this meeting started."

Mizusawa stood up and turned toward the three of us. The battle was over, and it had been fierce. I didn't understand what they were saying, but the intensity of their exchange was palpable.

Meanwhile, Mimimi ignored the whole battle and instead was scavenging around my room for porn DVDs. "Are they in here?" she murmured, pawing through my closet. "Where could they be?" Making herself a little too at home, I'd say.

Too bad for her, I'm the type who keeps everything in the Math folder on my laptop.

* * *

"A test of courage is going to be essential! I say basic is best!"

Mimimi cheerfully proposed her plan for getting Nakamura and Izumi together.

"I think you're right. If we don't do something like that, neither one of them will ever make a move." Mizusawa got on board.

I thought about contradicting them, but all I could come up with was something that would rock the foundation of the whole trip, like, *No, I think those two will get together on their own somehow. Let's believe in them*, so this time I decided to go along with Mimimi.

"Yeah. They say the suspension-bridge effect is powerful stuff."

"Exactly! Turn up the heat, and they'll jump into each other's arms! I knew you'd get it, Tomozaki!"

Hinami jumped in with Mimimi's cheerful mood. "Get the two of them alone, and they'll be inseparable!"

"Yeah! Ah, young love!" Mimimi said, bouncing off Hinami's words in return. The tidal wave of this conversation was something else. I was barely hanging on—hell, maybe I was already out—and I had to think about my assignment at the same time? I revved my brain into high gear.

"You ladies sure are enjoying yourselves!" Mizusawa laughed. "Now we just need to think of an excuse."

Hinami nodded. "I already checked with Yuzu, so there's no question how she feels."

"And Nakamu is totally into her! I can tell these things!"

"Anyone can tell that," Mizusawa said, getting in a quick jab.

"What?! No way?!"

"Yeah, I'm serious. Even you can tell, right, Fumiya?!"

"Yup, even me."

"Really?!"

Mimimi made a dramatic show of surprise. I was secretly pleased with myself for having joined in so smoothly with this snappy conversation, but I was also preparing myself for the next wave. Plus, I had to look for my chance to butt heads with Mizusawa again. To do that, I was going to have to ignore the need to ride the wave to a certain extent. Ahhh…too much to think about.

Or maybe the wave wasn't going to come, and I had to make it myself. *Um, like this?*

"We're having a barbecue, right?"

"Um, yeah."

"How about we give them some jobs where they'll end up alone together?"

Should I be making proposals?

"Hey, that's a good idea!" Mizusawa said. "Like have them make the fire or something!"

Yes! I succeeded in drawing out an answer to my own proposal that I could contradict! Based on some research I'd done in advance, I brought my argument into play.

"Or better yet…how about we have them cut up the ingredients?"

I didn't even miss a beat in the conversation.

"You think so?" Mizusawa asked directly, looking right at me.

Okay, better think of a reason…

"I—I mean, making the fire is a tough job, so I'm not sure we should leave it to those two…"

"Ha-ha-ha! Is that why? You may be right!" Mizusawa laughed. I'd ended up making fun of Izumi and Nakamura a little bit again. That seems to be the inevitable result when I'm thinking about arguing back at the same time.

Anyway, point two gained! Let's keep going—one more!

Or that was my plan, but the conversation was moving on without me.

"Something's bugging me," Mizusawa muttered as the strategy started to fall into place.

"What is it, young man?" Mimimi was being goofy again.

"Pretty soon we'll be third-year students getting ready for university entrance exams."

"You promised not to mention that…!" Mimimi's face turned white.

"That's not it, but…"

As Mizusawa rubbed his brow, Hinami spoke up from her spot next to him.

"You're saying we don't have much time to goof around, so we'd better make sure we get them together on this trip?" She grinned.

"Yeah…basically," Mizusawa said softly, looking away from her.

Aha! Looks like he's a lot more thoughtful than he seems on the surface… Is this my chance?

I took a deep breath. I mentally reviewed the tones I'd practiced on the voice recorder and the skills I'd stolen from Mimimi, Hinami, and even Mizusawa himself. That would allow my body to do the necessary work even if my mind was all tense and nervous.

"Hey, Mizusawa, you're not getting all mushy on us, are you?" I teased—lightly, with my best joking tone.

Mimimi giggled. "He is! I noticed the same thing! Are you embarrassed, Takahiro? What a good guy!"

As Mimimi added another hit, Mizusawa smiled.

"Ha-ha-ha, right? I am a good guy."

He pounded his chest comically.

Wow. He took our teasing and immediately turned it inside out to display his position as leader. The masterful skill of a normie.

Anyway, that made three points. Assignment completed.

"But I get what you mean! They're into each other, and they seem like such a perfect pair; it's a waste for them not to be together! And we can't stay young forever…" Mimimi pretended to cry, but part of her seemed serious.

"Yup," Mizusawa said, nodding solemnly.

Their exchange surprised me a little. I'd assumed that even though they were talking about getting Izumi and Nakamura together, the main point of the trip was to have fun. But apparently, everyone was serious about their goal.

Until recently, I assumed normies lived a happy-go-lucky life and never thought deeply about anything. Had I been mistaken? After all, the ones here with me thought very earnestly about their friends.

My enthusiasm for this whole becoming-a-normie thing just spiked a little.

* * *

Twenty or thirty minutes later, we'd hammered out all the details of our plan and were hanging around chatting.

"Anyway, right then Shuji's parents called him, and he had to go home."

"Ah-ha-ha-ha! That was perfect timing! I guess his parents really are strict!"

"Yeah. I mean, think about it. Shuji's a total dumbass, and he hates studying. He'd never get into Sekitomo High if his family wasn't hard-core about education."

"Very true!" Mimimi cackled with loud, over-the-top laughter.

The conversation was heating up over this story about how Nakamura had to go home just when he was about to get into a fight at the arcade with some guys from another school.

Hinami gave her own cute, sophisticated laugh before broadening the topic. "Shuji is usually so full of himself, but he can barely lift his finger against his parents. Wonder why."

"Well, I've never seen her in person, but from what I've overheard from his phone conversations…his mom's married to a gangster." Mizusawa mimicked slicing through the base of his right pinkie with his left pointer finger, indicating the infamous yakuza punishment.

"Yikes, don't do that! That was scary!" I said. I was done with my assignment, but I wanted to take the initiative to tease him a little more. Even as I was saying it, though, I could feel that my delivery was off.

"Really? But I'm telling the truth."

"I mean, gangster wives still have their pinkies."

There was no turning back now, so I dived in further. I was spiraling out of control.

Mizusawa just stared at me for a minute before finally saying, "Ha-ha-ha. Yeah, I guess so." His short, cynical laugh was followed by an uncomfortable-sounding comment.

I glanced over at Mimimi. She seemed confused.

"Uh, I mean, no..." Right then, I came back to my senses. I'd gotten carried away and said something weird. Hinami had told me to keep it to three times, and now I'd overdone it and screwed things up. What to do now? This was so embarrassing. *P-please don't look!*

I shut up for a minute, falling into a depression by that one small moment of awkwardness. I'm sure everyone was thinking I was one of those weirdos who makes awkward comments...and Hinami was giving me exasperated looks. *But at least I finished my assignment!*

To escape the discomfort of her gaze, I brought up a topic I'd memorized.

"Anyway, changing the subject...don't you guys think Erika Konno has been kinda grumpy lately?"

This prompted a strong response from Mimimi. "Oh yeah, I noticed that, too!!"

"She has been acting weird," Hinami said, nodding.

"She's probably annoyed because it looks like Yuzu is gonna take Shuji away from her."

"Definitely a possibility!" Mimimi said, latching onto Mizusawa's analysis.

Whew, I was out of the woods. Thank you, topic memorization. Guess I'd mastered the technique well enough to call on it in my hour of need.

After that, with disaster narrowly averted and my assignment done, I managed to introduce a couple more topics I'd memorized especially for this occasion and somehow remain part of the conversation. Since I wasn't attempting any more weird challenges, I was able to lie low for the rest of the day. My specialty.

Still, the old me wouldn't even have been able to imagine having an ordinary conversation with three normies—and not just any normies, three conversational masters. I felt like I'd achieved something.

More than that, though, probably the most surprising thing was that I actually enjoyed the conversation.

Around six, Mimimi looked at the clock on her phone and dropped her jaw.

"Shoot, I better get going! I'm supposed to go out with my grandma and the rest of my family for dinner tonight!"

Hinami checked her watch, too. "Really? Then should we all get going pretty soon?"

"Yeah, I was thinking we could get dinner at Jonathan's, but let's call it a day! We talked enough!"

"Ha-ha-ha, yeah, true," I said, nodding. I was out of memorized topics anyway.

"Oh, Tomozaki—I'll invite you to our LINE group, okay?" Hinami said in her fake voice. "We can use that for strategy meetings during the trip!"

"Oh, okay," I replied.

Mizusawa stood up and surveyed the group like he was our leader or something. "Okay, guys, let's get going. Don't forget anything here."

Mimimi saluted me. "Too bad I didn't find any DVDs in your room!"

"Are you still talking about that?" Hinami said with an exasperated but somehow also affectionate smile.

The four of us headed downstairs. I walked them outside, glancing at my sister as she enthusiastically invited them to come hang out again. She was practically swooning when Mizusawa said "Bye" to her.

And so the unbelievable normie meeting at my house ended. I went back inside and shut the door, and immediately my sister attacked me with a totally tactless question.

"Hey!! Why are you friends with all the cool people? Is the anti-nerd strategy working?"

Let me tell you something, dear sister. I may be aiming to move up the social hierarchy, but I'm not going to get rid of my nerdiness. My love for Atafami *is eternal.*

2

The EXP you need for each level up changes constantly

Two days had passed since the strategy meeting at my house.

As my train trundled along, I realized this felt like heading to school on the morning of finals. I was going to Shibuya, which is where the little independent theater that was playing the Andi movie is located. In other words, I was about to go see a movie with Kikuchi-san. I still couldn't believe it myself.

"And then, Mimimi… Yeah, and after that, Hinami had something to say about my clothes, too…"

I was flipping through my flash cards, doing one final review of the topics I'd memorized before it was time for the real thing. Part of me was just trying to escape reality. I'd practiced hard over the past couple of days of vacation and had my conversation points memorized almost perfectly, but it was tough not to feel anxious as the big moment approached. It was just like going over English flash cards before a test. Of course, in this case I was practicing things to talk about, not vocabulary.

For the first time in ages, I was wearing a mask so that I could warm up my facial muscles without anyone on the train noticing. Recently, I'd stopped feeling so nervous around normies, but right now I was insanely tense. I had a feeling if I didn't do some warm-ups, my face might freeze up completely. It goes without saying that I planned to take the mask off when I got to Shibuya.

The train pulled into Ukimafunado Station on the Saikyo Line, which apparently is number one on some ranking of stations that I don't get at all. From here on out, we'd be in Tokyo. I'd escaped Saitama, which proudly calls itself the eternal number three of the Kanto region. Never guessed my high school experience would include going to see a movie in Tokyo with a girl.

We were supposed to meet in front of the Hachiko statue at Shibuya Station at two. The Andi film started at two thirty. According to Hinami, it was best to see the movie first, then get a casual bite to eat and have a great conversation before going our separate ways. Love how she made "having a great conversation" sound like the easiest thing in the world. Anyway, though, the movie was first.

I puffed out my chest, tensed my butt muscles, flexed my face, and reviewed my conversation topics. As I focused on a full-body preparation, the train headed inexorably toward Shibuya.

How would this high-level quest end? My stomach hurt just thinking about it.

* * *

I'd been worried about getting lost along the way, so I ended up arriving at Shibuya early and getting to the Hachiko statue around one forty-five. I looked around. No sign of Kikuchi-san, but lots of other people. I've heard people from Saitama call Omiya a city, but it's nothing compared to real Tokyo. Even if you ignore the energy on the streets and the number of people, Tokyo just feels different. If Shibuya was a normie, then Omiya was a poser. Omiya was trying so hard, it was painful to witness.

Of course, if Toto-chan, the bronze statue of a baby squirrel outside the east exit of Omiya Station, found out I was having these thoughts, he'd chew me to death.

As I waited for Kikuchi-san, I silently begged Toto-chan's forgiveness. *I'm sure you'd beat out Ukimafunado Station, little squirrel.*

Suddenly, among the crowds of mostly young people, I saw a beam of light. Even from afar, I could make out the divine aura. I even thought I saw a magic square floating around it.

I squinted, and sure enough, it was Kikuchi-san.

She was wearing a light, long-sleeved black cardigan over a loose white shirtlike thing and a fairly trendy-looking dark-orange skirt that came just below her knees. Wonder why she was wearing long sleeves.

She saw me, too, and our gazes met unexpectedly. Even as her mysteriously sparkling eyes nearly shorted out my mental processor, I visualized Mizusawa, lifted the corners of my mouth, and waved casually. Internally, though, I was a total mess. *She actually showed up?!* Sure we'd agreed to see the movie together, but the reality of it hadn't sunk in for me. When I saw her in real life, right in front of me, my brain was overwhelmed by the realization that our date was about to begin, and my thoughts slowed to a snail's pace.

Kikuchi-san trotted over to me on her delicate legs. The pale skin on her neck, as unsullied as pure spring water flowing ceaselessly from a magnificent boulder deep in the mountains, reflected the summer sunlight too bright for my eyes. At that very moment, she was standing within a one- or two-meter radius of me.

"S-sorry…to make you wait," she said, her cheeks flushed, maybe from the heat, and her head tilted down slightly. Her upturned eyes joined forces with the summer mugginess to steadily melt my heart.

"Uh, no, not at all… I just got here. It isn't even two yet." I clammed up a little at first, but then I was fine. I had to stay focused on not stuttering.

"Oh, r-really…?"

"Yeah. W-well…should we go?"

"Um, yes!"

Concentrating on my tone so that it wouldn't betray my nervousness, I selected one of the lines I'd prepared in advance using image training.

"It's this way, right?" I said, taking a step toward the theater.

"Y-yes! …This way."

We both started walking. We were in the middle of a chaotic throng of people and noises. Kikuchi-san walked the tiniest bit behind me with dainty, calm steps. I felt like we were inside a small bubble of peacefully flowing time among all these people hurrying down the street. So she could use time magic and white magic. Wow. But I was still barely hanging on against my anxiety.

"…I—I sure am looking forward to the movie. I watched a preview, and it was really beautiful."

"Yes…I agree."

Kikuchi-san was replying to my conversation topics with broken answers, like she was holding back. This was different from the completely calm, sacred atmosphere of the library. Maybe she couldn't use her magic at will when she wasn't in a book elemental field. She had her hands locked in front of her, fidgeting with them. Was she nervous, or was she forming symbols with her hands as she prepared to activate her magic? Probably the latter.

I was struggling over which of my memorized topics to use when I suddenly remembered Hinami's advice to say something about the other person. "Hey, I was wondering... Why the long sleeves on such a hot day?"

Kikuchi-san pinched the sleeves of her cardigan. "Um...my skin is sensitive..."

"...Yeah?"

"I burn very easily..."

"Oh, um...really?" I stumbled over my response because her answer was so unexpected.

"...Yes. I put a lot of sunscreen on my face and neck, but still..."

Kikuchi-san's face was growing redder and redder as she spoke. *W-wait, is she getting sunburned as we speak...?*

That's about how the conversation went as we walked along. After a little while, we arrived at the theater.

"Ooh!"

As the phrase *independent theater* might suggest, the building was really small for a movie theater. There was a ticket booth out front and a hallway leading inside right next to it. Nestled into an alleyway, it felt like stepping out of the hustle and bustle of Shibuya and into another world. The mood was much more unique than the theaters inside big commercial complexes. *Why not comment on that?* After all, Hinami had said it was okay to talk about the place where you were, too.

"What a cool place."

Kikuchi-san smiled placidly and looked around. "Yes, it is... Oh!" Apparently noticing something, she trotted in that direction. The hallway was lined with posters for films based on Andi books. Most of the films had been made a few dozen years earlier, and the posters had a vintage feel that perfectly matched the atmosphere of the theater.

"Wow!"

The look in Kikuchi-san's eyes as she gazed at the posters wasn't the usual mysterious and magical sparkle but instead the glimmer of a child who had seen a toy she wanted. Soon after she lost herself in the first poster, she moved on impatiently to the next one. After staring at that one for a bit, she moved on down the line.

"Wow..."

Eventually, she made her way to every poster. She seemed to want to see them all at once, frustrated that she could only look at one at a time. I could tell how much she loved Andi's work just by watching her. It was very endearing.

Finally satisfied that she had seen enough, she trotted back over to me.

"...We're really going to see it on the big screen, aren't we?" She smiled excitedly up at me, standing closer than usual.

"Um, uh, yeah. You're right."

"Oh, s-sorry!"

She flushed and took a step back. For a second, the mood turned—not exactly uncomfortable, but the energy had gone down.

"...Should we get our tickets?"

"...Yes, good idea."

We got our tickets and our drinks, and then we went into the theater a little early and waited for the film to start. My heart was pounding, sitting next to her in the dark room. What should I do while we waited? I wondered if Kikuchi-san would glow in the dark. Looking over to check, I saw that was not the case. She was smiling in wide-eyed, gleeful anticipation, and she was hugging her bag with both arms as she gazed at the screen. Damn, she was cute.

A few minutes later, the film started.

* * *

Needless to say, I didn't get up the nerve to hold Kikuchi-san's hand during the climax of the film. Everything went fine, though, and afterward we went to a café near the theater for an early dinner. Kikuchi-san was eating a plate of loco moco with a fried egg, rice, and salad while I nervously worked my way through pasta with tomato sauce. For some reason, I'd been eating a lot of pasta lately.

"...Ah!" I muttered. I'd accidentally put way too much pasta on my fork. I was incredibly tightly wound, being alone at a café with Kikuchi-san, and it was making me scatterbrained. I was now stuck with a giant forkful of pasta in my hand. *Wh-what do I do?*

Kikuchi-san was quietly eating her loco moco, but every now and then, she glanced at me. Which meant that if I put the pasta back on the plate and rewound it on my fork, she might be able to tell I was nervous. I steeled my will and stuck the colossal forkful into my mouth all at once.

"...Erf."

"...?"

Kikuchi-san tilted her head at the weird noise I'd just made. But I think she noticed my valiant efforts to chew, and she quietly returned to her own meal.

...What the hell am I doing?

Once I swallowed, which took quite a while, I felt a pang of regret. To make up for my mistake, I decided to take the lead in bringing up a conversation topic.

"So...I was wondering how they were going to film the scene where the last snow grouse flies away. I wasn't expecting them to show the shadow!" I visualized myself expressing an earnest thought and gestured a little as I spoke, but I was careful not to overdo it. Sticking to Hinami's advice about creating a tone, I expressed my thoughts on the film in the hopes of canceling out that weird "erf."

Kikuchi-san listened with a smile on her face. "Hee-hee, you're right. That really turned into a great scene."

"Didn't it? Also..."

I continued on with a couple more of my thoughts. After all, my one strength is speaking my mind with total honesty.

Seriously, though? It was a good movie. I really loved the original book, so I was worried about what I'd say if the adaptation was shitty, but instead I'd been pleasantly surprised. It was weird; even though they'd changed the story here and there and added some new scenes, they managed to perfectly re-create the great atmosphere of the original. I guess total faithfulness to the original isn't always the best way to adapt a book to film.

After a while, though, I started to feel like I was dominating the conversation. Plus, it would be hard to keep talking about the movie for our whole meal, so I brought up something else.

"By the way, we talked a lot about Mimimi in the library last semester, right?"

"Huh? Oh right, we did. She seemed to be having a hard time."

"After that…" I told her the happy ending to that story. "And you were wondering about Hinami, too, right?"

"Yes, I was wondering why she always tried so hard."

"Yeah! I still don't know why, but…"

"But…?"

"Well, I've seen her in regular street clothes a bunch of times, but the other day we got together with some classmates, and she was wearing all things I'd never seen before. I mean, she even puts in a huge effort with her clothes."

"She has such strong preferences in every realm."

"Exactly! It really reminded me how true that was…" I kept introducing topics I'd memorized and expanding on them. "By the way, I hear Andi has a new book coming out."

"Yes, he does! I heard that it's not actually a new book, but a never-before-published manuscript of his was discovered… It's called *Kind Dogs Stand Alone*, right?"

"Yeah, that's it!"

"It's coming out on the twenty-first of this month!"

I was working really hard to keep the conversation going by bringing up topics that Kikuchi-san would perk up at. I still wasn't great at it, but after spending so much time with Mimimi and copying Mizusawa's techniques, I'd gained a decent command over finding ways to build on a talking point and respond to what the other person said. As long as I had a large stock of topics ready to go, I was able to get by with almost no awkward silences. In other words, I'd acquired the undeniably normie-ish skill of keeping things going in a one-on-one conversation by introducing a constant stream of topics.

Or so I thought.

We'd finished our meals, and the waiter had brought us black tea. Kikuchi-san looked at me searchingly for a minute before finally speaking.

"Tomozaki-kun, you're a mystery."

"…Huh? Wh-what's a mystery?"

Her sudden comment killed some of the momentum I'd built up while I was leading the conversation, and I ended up giving a confused response. I mean, Kikuchi-san is the mysterious one!

"It's hard to explain... I'm sorry if that was rude."

"Wh-what?"

Kikuchi-san looked down as if she was searching for words, pausing pensively for a moment. Then her pure, sparkling eyes met mine. "Tomozaki-kun," she began, "sometimes you're suddenly very easy to talk to...and sometimes...you're suddenly very hard to talk to."

"Um..."

For a second, my mind was in total chaos. Finally, I managed to get my brain running and process what she had said.

Basically. In so many words. Sometimes, I managed to do well, but my skill was nowhere near perfected. I thought I'd been such a smooth talker today, but I'd failed quite a few times, and Kikuchi-san had felt it difficult to respond. Damn, my confidence a minute ago was embarrassing. What was I thinking, an "undeniably normie-ish skill"? Idiot.

"R-really?" I said, trying not to show how upset I was as my thoughts washed over me. *Right. Don't get full of yourself over tiny achievements. At least wait until you know how to wind pasta on a fork. I wish I could disappear.*

Ten or fifteen minutes passed.

Kikuchi-san had told me I was hard to talk to sometimes, but that didn't mean I could just give up. That would only make it even harder for her, so I kept on with my topics and making conversation like I'd been doing before. Maybe if I gained some more EXP right now, I'd be easier to talk to.

"Well, should we get going?"

"Okay."

Having finished our tea, we left the café, walked back to the station, and got on the train together.

As the train rattled along, Kikuchi-san looked at me hesitantly.

"Thank you for inviting me to the movie today. I had a really good time."

I nodded, internally swooning over her thoughtful little phrase. "Me too. And the café was nice."

"Yes...the food was really good."

Kikuchi-san smiled. The conversation ground to a halt, and we endured another moment of silence.

I was about to find something else to talk about, when I heard Kikuchi-san say, "Um..."

"Yeah?"

"Uh...you know how I said you're hard to talk to sometimes..."

"Oh, uh-huh," I said, a little surprised. "Don't worry about it... I mean, I think you're right..." I honestly did.

"Um, that's not what I meant." Kikuchi-san blushed for some reason.

"It's not?"

"Um...well, I haven't talked to guys my age very much..." She was even redder now and stumbled over her words. "So...most of the time when I talk to guys, it's hard...but..."

"B-but what?"

"When I'm with you, sometimes it's really easy, and I can just...talk, which is a first for me..."

"...Oh." I was so surprised I couldn't produce a fluent answer.

"I mean...I said you were hard to talk to sometimes, but that's normal for me. It was surprising that it was ever easy at all, so...um..."

"Uh-huh?"

"What I said before, I didn't mean it in a bad way... I should have just said it was the first time I felt so at ease talking to a guy...and then you wouldn't have...felt ..." Her face was as red as a strawberry now, and she was looking down and away. "What I said before, I meant it in a really good way... It was very valuable to me..."

"Oh...okay." Even though I was still surprised, I felt my chest growing hot.

"So..."

"Yeah?"

Kikuchi-san looked me in the eye very earnestly. Her cheeks were flushed, and her eyes were a little moist. "So...I'd like to go out together again...like we did today..." Her fingers curled around the hem of her skirt.

There was no way I could give a light, offhanded answer to that. So once again I said what I was thinking.

"...O-of course!"

And that was the end of my movie date with Kikuchi-san.

* * *

On the way home from the station, I sent Hinami a LINE message saying I'd completed my date. Right away, a notification popped up saying she'd read it, and a second later she was calling. What a response time.

"...Hello?"

"So how did it go?"

I gave her a quick rundown.

"Huh. Well, it sounds like you hit a couple speed bumps, but overall I'd say it was a big success."

"Oh, okay..."

I managed a reply, even though I felt a little self-conscious. At the same time, I realized that I was walking along a lamplit street on a humid summer night talking to a girl in my class on the phone. It gave me a weird floating sensation.

"Still, even if she didn't mean it in a bad way, note that she did say you're hard to talk to. Think about why that is."

"Ngh, I knew you'd bring that up..." That was what I was the most worried about.

"I wasn't there, so I can't say for sure...but my guess is that you were afraid of silence and kept bringing stuff up, or maybe...the topics you'd memorized weren't a very good fit for her."

"Could be..."

The tough part about all this was that it wasn't enough just to memorize stuff and say it.

"Simply put, you need experience, and you need skills."

"Oof."

"If you have time to say 'Oof,' use that time to get started actually fixing the problem," she scolded.

"O-okay, okay. And how do I do that...?"

"It's obvious, isn't it?"

Resigned to my fate, I sighed. "More experience and training?"

"Hexactly."

Ultimately, that seemed to be the answer to everything.

"Well then, I'll just have to try again next time, right?"

"Right. The trip assignment is coming up, so stay positive."

"Is that a positive thing?"

To Hinami, the opportunity for an assignment is a good thing. I can't compete with that kind of ambition.

"Anyway, how about inviting her to see the fireworks next?"

"…Fireworks, huh?"

Yet another powerful, normie-associated word.

"Yeah. Invite her as soon as you get home. You can tack it onto a thank-you for today."

"That fast?"

"She already told you she wanted to go out again, so she can hardly turn you down if you ask her now. Once some time passes, things could get dicier…so I think it's best to make a plan ASAP."

"Oh yeah, guess you're right…"

Once again, Hinami's killer logic won me over.

"The Toda fireworks are probably the biggest around here."

"T-Toda…?"

"Yeah. Anyway, as long as you do it by the middle of the month, it's fine. I'll leave the details to you."

"Oh, okay."

Our conversation wrapped up just as I was getting home. When I got up to my room, I saw I had a LINE message from Hinami on my phone. It contained a link to a website listing the main fireworks shows around Saitama. I wasn't sure if she was being considerate or just cranking up the pressure, but I gave in and started composing a message to Kikuchi-san.

[*Thanks for today! The movie was great, and I had a good time.*

I was wondering, if you're free on the sixth, do you want to go to the Toda fireworks with me?]

I had no idea if that was good or not, but at least it was something.

"…Let's go!"

With a cheer to summon my courage, I tapped the SEND button, threw my phone onto my bed, and closed my eyes.

I'd asked her out again…to see the fireworks…

Modern civilization and technology allowed you to do a crazy thing like that with a single tap of your finger—kinda scary. As I waited for my racing heart to calm down, my phone vibrated.

"Shit!"

The surprise attack made my heart beat even faster. *If this keeps up, my heart's gonna be vibrating as fast as my phone.* I picked it up. Kikuchi-san had messaged me. I tapped the notification nervously.

[*I'm free on the sixth!*

I'd love to go to the fireworks!]

I smiled.

Hinami had said Kikuchi-san was slow to respond, so the lightning-quick reply was enough to completely shake me up. Even the simple words she'd sent gave off a fairylike aura. Doing my best to keep my head despite her overwhelming attractiveness, I started to compose a response.

[*Great, let's go then!*

Maybe we can decide on the time and stuff in a couple of days?]

[*Okay, sounds good!*]

This time her response came in twenty or thirty seconds, which shook me up even more. I closed the LINE app and collapsed facedown on my bed. I was done for. My energy was at zero. If her beautiful white magic had drained my power this much, I must be an undead... I closed my eyes.

[*So...I'd like to go out together again...like we did today...*]

A vision of the Kikuchi-san blushing rose behind my eyelids. A mixture of embarrassment and bashfulness and happiness washed over me, and before I knew it, I was drifting off to sleep. Despite that moment of peace, though, I had my job interview coming up in two days, and the day after that was the barbecue trip... *But for now, I just wanna forget everything...*

* * *

It was two days after the movie date and one day before the trip. Before long, I'd be surrounded by normies for more than twenty-four hours straight for a major event, but right now I was nervous about something else.

I was standing in front of the karaoke place with my résumé in my bag.

Yes, I was about to have my interview. I'd lost count of how many events I'd survived just since vacation started. They all were helping me grow in some way, though, so it wasn't a waste. I was still feeling motivated.

I went into the karaoke place. The girl working there welcomed me apathetically, then yawned. Seriously? Trial by fire.

Her bleached wavy shoulder-length hair was tucked behind one ear. She looked around my age.

"Um, I have a job interview at ten. My name is Fumiya Tomozaki."

"Oh, they're waiting for you. Wait here a minute, 'kay?" she said in a monotone before disappearing into the back. *Not much enthusiasm for the job, huh...?*

A guy in his midthirties came up from the back. He was tall, fairly muscular, and imposing.

"Hi. Tomozaki-kun, right?"

"Uh, yes!"

"I'm Yanagihara, the manager here. Follow me!" he said briskly, leading me to a room to get the interview started. "Okay, first of all..."

For an interview, it was fairly informal. He asked me stuff like, "How many days a week can you work?" and "Have you ever had a job before?" and "How long do you plan to keep working?" Aside from that, we basically chatted about stuff not directly related to work, like my plans for the summer and whether I was involved in any clubs. I'm fairly sure I managed to get through it without any major mess-ups by using the techniques I'd cultivated so far to control my tone for clear, concise conversation.

More importantly, the difficulty level was relatively low compared to being tossed into a gaggle of normies or talking to a girl at a café. I wasn't absolutely certain I got the job, but as far as surviving the immediate situation, I think I squeaked through with my usual tricks. Guess that means I'm at the point where I can manage something like this. Actually, it's easier to talk to an older person than to someone my own age because there are more predetermined formalities.

"That's it for the interview! I'll get in touch later to let you know if you've got the job or not."

"Great! Thanks so much!"

Yanagihara-san and I left the room together.

"Hey, is that Fumiya?"

"Huh?"

I turned toward the voice and found Mizusawa standing there dressed in a staff uniform.

"Hey, dude, what are you doing here? Wait, were you the one scheduled for an interview today?"

"Is this a friend of yours, Mizusawa?"

"We're in the same class at school!"

"Oh, you go to Sekitomo, too? Wow. Tomozaki-kun, did you know he was working here?"

"No..."

Something occurred to me. Hinami was the one who suggested I apply here. Once again, she'd set me up for a gratuitous surprise...

"Well, that's a coincidence!"

"Y-yeah, it sure is..." I smiled ironically.

"Looking forward to working together, Fumiya... If he got the job?"

"Hey, you're asking me that here? Well, I did get the impression that he'd be able to interact professionally with our customers, so I was planning to offer him the job..."

"Hear that, Fumiya? Nice."

"Huh? Oh, great!"

The manager's positive evaluation set me reeling, and it was all I could do to keep up with this tsunami of a conversation. Oblivious to all that, Mizusawa kept talking.

"Hey, I get off in half an hour, so why don't you do some solo karaoke or something and wait for me. We can grab a bite to eat afterward."

"Uh, um..."

"Wait a second now, Mizusawa. You still have an hour and a half left!"

"Dang, you got me. But it's so dead today—can't I get off early? Literally nobody came while you were doing the interview. If you don't cut back on your labor costs, the area manager is gonna get mad at you again!"

"Uh...if you put it that way... Boy, you always have a comeback ready..."

"Which means—I'll see you soon, Fumiya!" Mizusawa punched me lightly on the arm.

"Uh, okay, got it."

Helpless against his momentum, I nodded, and Mizusawa disappeared down the hallway to do his janitorial duties. *Damn, the conversation really accelerated when multiple people were involved...*

"I never would have guessed you were a classmate of Mizusawa's. He's a fast talker, that one. A real troublemaker."

"Ha-ha-ha...very true."

"So what do you want to do? You gonna sing for a bit?"

"Uh, well...I did say I would."

"Ah-ha-ha, so you did. And I did say you got the job, so the job is yours. From now on, I'm your manager. Got it, Tomozaki?"

"Um, yes, sir!"

His sudden shift to a more authoritative tone caught me off guard.

"Uh, this is where we check people in. Watch how I do it, okay? Since you'll be working with us, you get an employee discount. Half off. Make sure you earn it, okay?"

"Y-yes, sir! Thank you very much!"

"Uh, like I said in the interview, everyone tends to quit right after summer vacation, so I'd like to finish training you by then... Can you start training in the middle or end of August?"

"Yes!"

That's how I ended up getting the job and singing for half an hour while I waited for Mizusawa. Aside from the fact that my first-ever karaoke experience ended up being solo, all was going well.

* * *

"Yeah...glad I decided to do this by myself."

I was alone in the little room learning by trial and error. I'd never even touched a karaoke machine before.

"Okay, so this button ends the song...and there are a bunch of ways to search."

The interface was intuitive, so I figured it out pretty quickly, but if I'd had to explain it to a customer without ever doing it myself, I probably would have panicked. *Close call.*

"And this is…"

Just as I started messing around with the main device, there was a knock on the door just before a female employee came in.

"Oh, hi, nice to meet you… Er, again, I guess."

"Huh? Oh right, hi again."

Turning toward the monotonous voice, I saw the same girl I'd talked to when I first arrived. After my awkward response to her greeting, she apathetically plopped down in the chair across from me. *Uh, isn't she in the middle of her shift? Is she allowed?*

"My name is Tsugumi Narita. I work here part-time. Made it through the interview, huh?"

"Yes, and it's nice to meet you! I'm Fumiya Tomozaki. I'll be starting here soon." I introduced myself in as cheerful a tone as possible. I'm not half-bad at polite conversations.

"You're a high school second-year, right, Tomozaki-san?" Slumped in the chair without a hint of shame, she continued in her monotone voice.

"Yes. I'm in my second year."

"I'm in my first year, so you don't have to be so polite with me."

She didn't waste any time in telling me to drop the formalities. This just got a lot harder. *Wait a second; things are moving fast for a bottom-tier character. I'm alone in a small room with a girl I've just met. I know I've been talking to girls a lot more lately, but this is on a different level.* For the moment, I tried to remember how I talked with Mimimi and Izumi.

"Oh, okay, got it… By the way, Narita-san, aren't you working right now?" I wasn't sure what to make of this girl who had just plopped down in here like she owned the place, so my only choice was to deploy a basic strategy and make the other person into the topic of conversation.

"Oh, that's not a problem. The boss was the one who told me to come say hi to you, and I'm sure he knew I'd sit down in here for a couple minutes."

She flopped over the table as she talked, glancing at her phone to check the time. She just did whatever she wanted—what was her deal? As I looked at her, I mentally reviewed my assignment for getting to be friends with Mizusawa—teasing and arguing back.

If that was the secret to establishing equal relationships, should I be

NA

doing it right now, too? Hinami had told me to get better at independent thinking…so why not take the initiative and try it out? I swallowed, planned out what to say, and adjusted my voice.

"Narita-san…are you a troublemaker?" I asked in a teasing tone.

She giggled. "Busted already, huh? Yeah, I'm basically a deadbeat."

"Ah…ha-ha-ha."

I hadn't expected her to agree with me right away, so instead of saying something back, I just laughed cynically. *Pfft.* Things never go smoothly.

"But I always sit no matter how many times he tells me not to, so I think he'll probably give up soon."

Narita-san lifted her head from the table, played with the ends of her hair, and gave me a silly smile. What was with her powerful determination…?

"You mean the boss…?"

I thought back pityingly to the manager I'd just met. Suddenly, Narita-san let out an "Oh," sat up, and looked at me gravely.

"Wh-what?"

"Are you hungry?"

"Huh?"

"Wanna order something?"

My mind froze momentarily at her boldness.

"The fries here are always good. And they come with two sauces. Let's get one salted cod roe sauce, okay? And you can choose the other one."

"N-Narita-san, are *you* hungry…?"

"Oh no, I'm mostly ordering it for you. When I take a break from work and stop by again, I might want to have a few bites if there's any extra. I'm not a *total* pig." She pouted, as if my question was something rude.

"Uh, um…?"

I was thinking about how to question her logic—making me order something so that she could have the leftovers when *she* was the hungry one—when she leaned toward me and said, "Oh, I was meaning to ask you…"

Come on now! This is moving way too fast for me. I haven't trained enough for this! "Wh-what?"

"Do you really go to the same school as Mizusawa?" A hint of excitement suddenly crept into her listless attitude.

"Um, yeah, I do."

"Really? Can I ask you something, then?"

"…Uh, what?"

She leaned forward with a gleeful smile. "Well… I'll get to the point. Does he like anyone right now?" she asked, her voice lowered like this was really important. She had something up her sleeve, I could tell.

"…I'm not sure."

"Does that mean there is someone?"

"N-no…"

I remembered my very short conversation with Hinami on the topic and that I'd been wrong about their relationship. Which meant Mizusawa wasn't seeing anyone…didn't it?

"Uh…well, I haven't heard anything in particular…so maybe no?"

Narita-san nodded pensively a few times. "Aha, I see… Thanks so much for the intel!"

She looked satisfied. I couldn't tell how she really felt, but I figured this might be a good chance to mess with her again. I came up with something to say and made my voice very serious.

"Does this mean what I think it means? Do you…have a crush on him?"

I wasn't quite up to teasing a girl I'd just met, so I hesitated a little midsentence. Still, I managed to sound teasing enough. Narita-san giggled a little.

"Um, well…Mizusawa-senpai is pretty hot, so a bunch of girls here like him. That's why I thought it would be fun to ask…"

"Oh, really."

"As for me…if I had to say whether I genuinely like him, well, I'm not head over heels."

"…Oh yeah?"

Her silly expression convinced me she wasn't hiding anything. "He is cute, though," she added.

With that, she glanced at her phone, let out a gasp like she just realized how late it was, shot to her feet, and headed for the door with deadly seriousness.

"I better get going. It'll be close, but if I leave right now, I shouldn't get in trouble!"

"Oh, okay."

...What's with that calculation?

"Thanks for the valuable intel," she said, once again in a monotone. With a sharp salute, she left the room.

She'd had me wrapped around her finger with her free and easygoing ways. I felt like a storm had just blown through. And that thing about him being cute...

Yeah, Mizusawa was a handsome guy.

* * *

"Sorry to keep you waiting, dude!" Mizusawa came out from the back after finishing his shift and changing into street clothes.

"Hey." I greeted him with a casual smile. Pretty soon these little smiles would be second nature. At least, I'd like to think so.

"See you later," he said on his way out.

The manager, who was working behind the register, smiled cheerfully.

"Yup, see you next time. You too, Tomozaki."

"Yes, looking forward to it!"

Narita-san came out from the back room. "Bye, guys!"

"Bye."

"Bye," I jumped in.

"Don't slack, Gumi," Mizusawa said.

"I won't! Sheesh," Narita-san responded amiably. What was "Gumi" all about? Maybe it came from her first name, Tsugumi?

The boss and Narita-san waved as Mizusawa and I left Karaoke Sevens together.

"Let's go!" Mizusawa said, heading toward the station.

"Wh-where?"

"There's a lot of places around here. Anything you feel like eating? Are you even hungry?"

"Uh, yeah, a little."

"Tenya okay with you? I stop there a lot on my way home."

"Okay!"

I was getting more used to deploying the Izumi-style "Okay." I think that as long as I have enough of these smooth templates ready to use when the opportunity presents itself, I'll be able to have normal conversations.

We headed toward the Tenya tempura restaurant near the east exit of the station, walking side by side.

"So why'd you decide to get a job all of a sudden? Short on cash?"

"Yeah, basically." I thought for a second. "With the trip and everything..."

"Ha-ha-ha. That's a heavy hit."

"Right? Ten thousand yen is a lot for a high school kid."

"I feel ya, man." The conversation was going along smoothly. Amazing. We sounded like friends. "But..."

Just as Mizusawa started saying something, we reached the restaurant. He took the lead, opening the door and going in, and I followed him. We sat down and ordered.

"That sure was a coincidence, though," I said, introducing a topic myself. With Mizusawa, that alone was enough to make me nervous.

"A coincidence, huh? Yeah, guess so," he said halfheartedly. That made me slightly anxious, since I suspected Hinami had set the whole thing up.

"Okay, be honest with me," he said, resting his elbows on the table and pointing at my face. "Is the job part of your anti-geek strategy?"

"Uh..."

Mizusawa had already told me he thought I was reading books on how to ditch my geeky persona, which was almost exactly the same thing my sister had said to me. He knew I was trying to change some things about myself; he hadn't uncovered Hinami's contributions, but he was sharp. And now he thought the job was part of it all. He'd hit the nail on the head; I didn't know how to reply.

Suddenly, he burst out laughing.

"Huh?"

"Dude...even if I'm right, don't be so obvious about it."

"No...I mean, uh," I said, remembering my reaction. "...Y-you're right." Now that he pointed it out, I had to admit, responding with "Uh" was pretty damning.

"The way you talk has changed a lot. I'm sure you've been working hard, but you've got a long way to go when it comes to playing it cool."

His comment was a little harsh, but his tone was so cheerful it didn't come off as unkind. He was so good at keeping it light when he messed with people. I was looking for my own chance to get in a jab at him, but he didn't leave many opportunities.

"Lay off!" I said, keeping it equally light.

"Seriously, though..." He was still smiling, but his eyes were serious. "You don't mess around, do you?"

"Huh?"

That was a surprise, coming from him.

"It was the same when you got into it with Erika and with your anti-nerd strategy and with *Atafami*. From what I could tell, you were involved in that thing with Mimimi's speech, too, weren't you?"

"Uh..."

"Ha-ha! Gotcha again."

"Yeah." I started laughing, too. *Gotta admit, that was bad.*

"So I was right, huh? You're too easy to read, Fumiya."

Since he already had me pegged anyway, I decided to fess up.

"What can I say...? I wanted to help Mimimi win..."

For some reason, Mizusawa blinked at me dramatically in shock. Then he tilted his head and smiled for a second. "You mean you wanted to beat Aoi?"

"Yeah, well."

"...Huh."

Mizusawa looked down and swished his ice around noisily in his cup. His long eyelashes hid his languid eyes. I'm sure he had some thoughts of his own. *Damn, he looks way too much like a picture of a guy drinking whiskey on the rocks. That* is *water in there, right?* As I was examining his cup, the waiter returned with my tempura over rice and Mizusawa's deluxe version of the same dish. Even eating at a cheap tempura restaurant, we were on different levels.

"I'm impressed you went so hard to beat her. What was driving you?" he asked calmly as he split his disposable chopsticks apart. I thought for a minute.

"I'm not sure how to explain exactly, but...it's like I didn't want to let her beat me in the game..."

"Game?" He stared at me blankly as he chewed his shrimp tempura. Back to his same old rhythm.

"Oh, I mean, the student council election felt like a kind of game, in a sense…," I bumbled as I picked up a piece of fried winter squash.

Mizusawa nodded. "I can see that."

"R-really?" I got a little excited; I wasn't expecting him to understand. Also, the squash was really good.

"Oh yeah. But you take losing that seriously even when it's just a game?"

"Huh? I take it *more* seriously when it's a game."

He made an impressed sound. "You're a go-getter, aren't you?" he commented, taking a bite of rice mixed with sauce.

I had a few thoughts of my own, though. I mean, look at Mizusawa…

"But what about you? You're great at talking to people, and you don't mumble… You must have put some effort into all that."

"Oh yeah? What kind of effort?" he pressed.

"Huh? Such as? Uh, copying people who're good talkers, or…"

In my rush to say something, I mentioned one of my own strategies.

"So you mean…?" Mizusawa grinned. "You do stuff like that?"

Shit. He baited me. "Uh…"

It was out before I could stop myself. Mizusawa laughed again. "You really are an open book!"

"You got me on that one…"

"Hey, it's your fault for falling for it! Seriously, though, I don't copy anyone!"

"Huh, r-really?"

And he was this good? I guess normies were naturally blessed…

"I've always been the type who caught on quick to stuff. I just know which buttons to press, I guess? Call me a genius!" he joked.

"Okay, but you do seem like the type…"

What was all my work for, then? All this time spent memorizing and copying, and I was still nowhere near Mizusawa. He leaned toward me, smiling his own slightly sadistic smile.

"The real question is, who have you been copying?"

"Uh, it's…"

Was he really asking? Now what do I do? I briefly flailed for an answer before deciding he'd figure it out eventually anyway. Might as well confess.

"Uh, a lot of people but mainly…y-you."

"…What?" For a second, he gaped at me like I'd genuinely caught him off guard. Then he cackled. "Who comes out and *says* that to a guy?"

"Well, you asked…and you'd know if I was lying, right?"

This time his smile looked exasperated. "You are *so* weird, man."

"A-am I?"

From my perspective, I'm so mediocre I get buried in the crowd.

"How can I put this? For instance…," he said, peering into my eyes. "Hinami and me, we're smart through and through. Know what I mean?"

"Smart through and through?"

How was that different from plain old smart? And if it was the same, wasn't it conceited of him to say it himself? He was making me feel the same way Hinami did.

I waited for him to go on.

"And then you have people like Shuji and Yuzu and Takei, who are idiots through and through."

"Idiots through and through… Okay, I wanted to ask, but how's that different from a regular idiot?"

"No, it's basically the same, but…"

"But?"

Mizusawa frowned. "I think you're a smart idiot."

"…What's that supposed to mean?" It was a fine line between compliments and insults sometimes, and I couldn't tell which this was.

"When I watch what you do and how you think, a lot of the time I think you're smart…but actually, you're an idiot."

"Okay, you're definitely insulting me."

"No, I'm not!" As usual, his joking self-defense was totally without venom. Yup, he was a top-tier character.

"R-really? That's a compliment?"

"Just forget about that for now."

"How am I supposed to forget about it?!" I shot back cheerfully. *Pretty smooth, eh?*

"Ah-ha, is that the Mizusawa-style talk I've heard so much about?"

"S-stop already…!"

Mizusawa's grin was like an attack that left me inflicted with embarrassment, and the strength immediately drained from my words. He was a strong one. Never left himself exposed. Messed with me all the time. A classic normie.

"Ha-ha! Hey, by the way, did you pack yet for tomorrow?" He breezily changed the topic. He had the role of leader in an iron grip for this conversation.

"Yeah, I put what I thought I might need in my backpack." Specifically, the black one Hinami gave me. In hindsight, I would have been in trouble without that.

"Oh yeah? Wonder if those two will end up getting together tomorrow."

"Wh-who knows…?"

We talked about the trip for a while, and before too long, dinner was over.

We walked back to the station together and parted ways on the Saikyo Line platform, since our houses were in opposite directions.

"See ya later, man."

I pulled myself together to deliver a short reply in a smooth normie fashion.

"Yup, see ya."

Nailed it. I'm ashamed to be proud of something so small, but progress is progress! I took the train to Kitayono, headed out of the station, and pulled out my phone. [*Got the job*], I wrote to Hinami on LINE. And then: [*You set me up for a weird surprise, didn't you?*]

A few minutes later, she wrote back, and she knew exactly what I was talking about: [*You get to test yourself in a new environment, you make some money, and you improve your relationship with Mizusawa. Three birds with one stone, right?*]

She doesn't give an inch, does she? I was right; she did it on purpose…

Okay, Hinami, I get that you want to be efficient, but can you stop with the gratuitous surprises?

3

Multiplayer games have their own special appeal

Finally, the day of the barbecue trip arrived.

I wasn't waiting at Kitayono Station for long before Mimimi arrived.

"You sure are early, Tomozaki! Should we get going?"

"Okay!"

We'd all agreed to meet at Ikebukuro Station, but earlier in the morning, Mimimi had suddenly texted me on LINE and suggested we take the train together, so we ended up doing that. It was a situation typically reserved for normies, but I wasn't too nervous. I was fairly used to hanging out with Mimimi, and at this point, I even felt slightly at home. What an incredible change that was.

As usual, Mimimi was simply dressed in jeans and a T-shirt, but she managed to look stylish anyway. Once again, I realized how attractive she was to pull that off. It was just like her, too, to be carrying a sporty backpack stuffed to the gills.

We charged our train passes with enough money for the round-trip journey and went through the ticket gates.

"Another hot day again, huh?"

"Yeah."

"Perfect weather for a barbecue!"

"...You think so?"

Mimimi snapped a finger upward. She pointed at the ceiling, but I think she meant to indicate the sky. "Obviously, Brain!! The meat awaits us!"

"Oh right."

I've heard people say hot days are barbecue weather before, but it never made sense to me. I'm not exactly an outdoorsy type, so personally I try to avoid the sun on hot days...

It wouldn't do me much good to say that, though, so I changed the subject.

"A-anyway, I wonder how everything will go."

"Me too! Hum, hum, shall our stratagem with Yuzu and Shuji meet with success or failure?" Mimimi pretended she was stroking an imaginary mustache.

"Um…well, I think it all depends on Nakamura."

"Ah-ha-ha-ha! True! Nakamu can be such a wimp sometimes." Mimimi energetically bounced her full backpack up and down, laughing as she placed her hands on her hips. *Where'd the mustache go? Or are we past that already?*

"So do you have a good plan for us this time, Brain?"

Mimimi leaned in close and peered cheerfully into my face. Her perfectly formed eyes and nose were right next to mine. *Wow, she has really good skin.* I reflexively turned my eyes away.

"Um…that stuff isn't exactly my strong suit."

"So modest! You were perfect during the election!" She winked and poked her finger into the air.

"Oh, no, I meant anything involving romance…"

"Ah yeah! You definitely have a point there!"

"Ouch."

"Ah-ha-ha-ha!"

We were joking around as the train carried us toward Ikebukuro. Talking to Mimimi felt natural now; the conversation flowed so smoothly I didn't even have to think about it. She knew I was a gamer and adjusted how she talked to me accordingly, but most important of all, her laughter was genuine, which made me enjoy myself, too. All we were doing was standing on a train talking, but I wasn't bored at all. *H-hey, is this…friendship?!*

"That reminds me. I had an interview the other day for a part-time job, and it turns out Mizusawa works at the same place."

"No way! What a coincidence. So now you guys are gonna be work buddies?"

I introduced a couple more topics, and pretty soon we were at Ikebukuro. Mimimi and I joined the huge crowd of people getting off the train.

"By the way, Tomozaki...," Mimimi began a little shyly as we walked along the platform.

"Yeah?"

"Um, it's just..." She looked away and scratched her cheek. "I wanted to thank you for everything recently! You really...saved my butt. So thank you again!"

"Oh, uh, yeah, it was nothing."

That caught me off guard. I felt my face growing hot with embarrassment.

"When I thought about it, I realized you really did a lot for me! You were like...my hero! I mean it. Um, yeah! That's what I wanted to say! Let's go!"

With that very uncharacteristic speech, she sped ahead of me down the platform.

"Uh, yeah, okay. Wait!"

As I hurried to catch up, I thought about what she'd said. No one had ever thanked me for anything so directly. A pleasant warmth spread through my chest.

I'm not quite sure how to put it, but I guess I was glad I'd made the effort to involve myself in other people's lives.

* * *

We'd all agreed to meet a short walk from the JR Ikebukuro exit, near the Seibu Ikebukuro Line ticket gate. From there, we were going to take the Seibu Ikebukuro Line to Hanno Station and transfer to a bus that would take us to the campsite. When Mimimi and I got to the meeting place, Hinami, Mizusawa, and Nakamura were already there.

"Hey."

"'Sup."

Nakamura and Mimimi exchanged casual normie-ish greetings. Everyone else followed their lead with brief "Heys." I rode the greeting wave by copying them.

"So we're waiting for Takei and Yuzu again, huh? Both repeat offenders," Mizusawa said.

"Yeah, they're always late! I know they read the LINE message I sent this morning. They probably just aren't worried about being on time…" Hinami checked her phone while she talked.

After a few minutes, the two of them arrived. Izumi was first.

"Geez, you guys are early! Am I the last one?!"

"Nope, still waiting for Takei."

"Huh?" She glanced around. "Oh yeah, no Takei…"

H-had she forgotten he was coming…? He hadn't been invited to the strategy meeting either… Oh man, Takei…

A few minutes later, the man arrived.

"Shit! Am I last?! Anyway, let's take a photo to get things rolling!"

With that slapdash attempt to distract us from his lateness, he pulled up the camera on his phone, herded everyone together, and snapped a couple of selfies.

"Okay! I'll post these on Twitter!"

What planet was this guy living on? I felt sorry for him but also totally lost.

We piled onto the Seibu Ikebukuro Line and headed to Hanno Station, chatting about nothing much on the way. From there, we were going to take a forty-minute bus ride to a stop near the campsite.

The Nakamura-Izumi strategy was about to begin.

The key here was where we all sat. The first step in our plan was to have the two of them sit next to each other. Incidentally, there were four guys (Nakamura, Mizusawa, Takei, and me) and three girls (Hinami, Izumi, and Mimimi) on the trip. That made seven of us altogether, so if we sat in pairs, one person would end up sitting alone. I figured it would be okay if that person was me. Anything for the cause!

When we got on the bus, I saw the back row was already full, so we were indeed going to pair off. We'd discussed several strategies for making sure they sat together. Hinami was the first to take action.

"Let's sit here, Takahiro!"

With that, she breezily plopped into a window seat and gestured for Mizusawa to sit next to her. The idea was for the girls to tell the guys where to sit, leaving Nakamura until the end so he ended up with Izumi. Mimimi moved next.

"Hey, Brain, mind if I take the window seat?"

She sat down behind Hinami and Mizusawa.

What?! She named me? Swallowing my surprise, I sat down next to her. *Damn, she's close.*

All Izumi had to do now was tell Nakamura to sit next to her! *Sorry, Takei, but you'll deal, right? You're used to this stuff. After all, you weren't even invited to the strategy meeting.*

"Um…," Izumi mumbled, turning red. "I guess, um…Takei."

"Huh?" Nakamura said.

"Hey, Takei! Let's sit here!"

"Seriously? Okay!"

Seemingly oblivious to what was going on, he smiled happily at being chosen. He plopped down next to her, said something like, "Selfie time!" and snapped a picture with his phone. Was Takei genuinely an idiot? Well, I suppose since he hadn't been told about the plan…

"Gonna post this on Twitter!"

He started messing with his phone. What was with him? He was in his own little happy world. Meanwhile, we were all absorbed in our plan.

Grimacing, Nakamura sat down alone behind Izumi and Takei. I leaned out into the aisle to look at him and caught his sharp gaze pointed at me.

"What?"

"N-nothing."

Growing inexplicably apologetic, I shrank back into my seat.

That was how Izumi's shyness caused Nakamura to sit alone, leading to the unbelievable failure of the grand bus seating strategy. This was not going well. *Come on, Izumi; how about you get with the plan?*

As we rode along, the seating arrangement stopped mattering because everyone was talking with the people in front of them and behind them. In that sense, the collapse of the seating strategy had probably resolved itself; it would have been the same even if Nakamura and Izumi were sitting next to each other. As for me, I managed to keep up with the conversation but not to push forward the couple strategy. Two assignments at once was still beyond me.

The bus pulled up at our stop. We had to walk about five minutes from there.

"Ooh, we're definitely in the mountains now," Izumi said, blocking the sun with her hand. The glitter on her nails sparkled in the sun. True enough, the road was paved, but there were trees on either side. *Ah, nature.*

"It's so hot." Nakamura's scowl alone was enough to make me feel intimidated. As he'd pointed out, the sun was high overhead and getting hotter by the minute. The trees might be providing a little relief compared to the city, but it was still superhot.

"Okay, should we get going?"

Holding an oddly shaped branch she'd picked up, Mimimi took the lead and started walking.

"Mimimi, wrong way!" Hinami wasted no time in scolding her.

"What?! Really?"

Mimimi swept her error under the rug with a giggle. *Oh, Mimimi.*

* * *

Following Hinami's directions, we made it to the campground. It was pretty big and surrounded by trees. According to the map posted up front, there were two areas: a big open field and a gravelly riverbed. The log cabins we'd be staying in were in the field. The plan was to have the barbecue by the river and then go to the cabins afterward. The guys and girls were staying in separate cabins. Totally kosher.

"Okay, guys, ten thousand each!"

Mizusawa collected the cash and used some of it to pay the camping fees. The rest would go toward other expenses, and we'd get back anything that was left over at the end. Very efficient. These guys were pros.

Inside the campground, a bunch of groups were already putting meat on the grill. The field was basically like an enormous park without many amenities aside from benches and little shelters, so people had set up canopies and parasols to shield themselves from the sun. There were families and university students and kids our age.

"Wow, it's already packed! We'd better find a spot quick!" Izumi pranced around excitedly.

I almost wanted to do the same. It *was* exciting. *Now just take that excitement and direct it toward Nakamura, Izumi.*

"First things first," Nakamura said, heading over to the building labeled CAMP CENTER in the middle of the field. The rest of us followed to rent a barbecue set: a grill packed with charcoal, some tongs, enough food for the seven of us, a chef's knife, and a cutting board. With the canopy, we had a lot of stuff to carry. Now this was starting to feel like a barbecue. We lugged everything down to the riverbank and started to set up. It was a little cooler down there, probably thanks to the water nearby.

"All right, everyone, time for job assignments!" Hinami declared in a theatrical impression of a manager.

"Yes, ma'am!" Takei chirped in response. Hinami was supposed to give Izumi and Nakamura a job together. Knowing her, she'd probably pull it off with ease.

"First, Yuzu and Shuji…I'd like you to wash and cut the vegetables."

"What?!"

"Gotcha."

Izumi was caught off guard while Nakamura responded with imposing confidence. Hinami had boldly named the two of them right off the bat. Very like her.

I figured the rest of the assignments didn't matter much—until I heard them.

"Setting up the tent and table will be a lot of work, so let's have Takahiro, Takei, and Mimimi on that."

"Got it."

"We're on it."

"Okay!"

The three of them responded…which meant… *Wait a second!*

"That leaves me and Tomozaki-kun to get the fire started. All righty, let's get to work, guys!"

Looked like I was working with Hinami. Did she want to have a meeting or something?

Everyone cheerfully took up their positions and started in on their tasks under the hot midsummer sun.

* * *

"What's this about?" I asked Hinami, using my typical meeting tone. We were working far enough away from everyone else that they couldn't hear us. The real point of having everyone spread apart, of course, was so Nakamura and Izumi could talk without being overheard. All I could tell from this far away was that Takei was monkeying around and taking a bunch of photos of the other two setting up the canopy. Like I said, he was on his own planet.

"What's what about?" Hinami frowned.

"I thought you paired us up because you wanted to have a meeting about something."

"...Nope."

"Really?"

That was a surprise. She didn't want to talk about anything special? Then why were we working together?

"Um, then why?" I asked, feeling a little shy now.

"Well, I put Nakamura and Yuzu together according to our strategy, correct?" Hinami answered coldly. "And then, since the canopy is a tough job, I chose Mizusawa for his leadership skills, Takei for his physical strength, and Mimimi because she would fit in easily. I wanted to do the fire myself because if you mess that up, we can't do anything at all. You were left over, so you naturally ended up with me."

"...Oh." I sighed at her cold logic. *Typical.*

"Also, I get tired of putting on an act all the time," she added in a barely audible voice.

"Huh."

"...What?" She shot me a disgruntled glance.

"Nothing... I'm just surprised to hear you get tired of anything."

"Obviously. I'm only human."

"Now that you mention it, I guess you are..." I nodded. I'd almost forgotten.

"But it is a good idea to have a meeting. I still haven't told you today's assignment, after all." Hinami stared at the piece of charcoal she was twirling around with the fire tongs.

"An assignment? The general goal is for me to make some guy friends, right?"

"Yes. That it is. Also, I want you to get more conversation EXP. Don't forget that Fuka-chan said you're hard to talk to."

"Oh...right."

As I reflected on that particular comment again, my mood fell a little. I really had thought I was doing a good job making conversation.

"That said, just staying here overnight is gonna net you a lot of EXP, and it'll be a confidence booster, too. I think you'll be able to complete the assignment just by acting naturally."

"Huh... So as long as I actively try to make conversation, I don't have any other assignments?"

"Gaining EXP is the biggest thing. But while you're doing that, I also want you to do something else."

"Like what...?"

"Mess with the person you're talking to or contradict them, same as before."

"...Oof."

I shrank at the thought of repeating an assignment I'd struggled with. Hinami snorted.

"Three times—with Nakamura."

For a moment I was struck dumb.

"With *Nakamura*?!"

I barely managed to keep the volume of my voice down. Hinami nodded with satisfaction.

"If I don't make your assignments progressively harder, what's the point?" She sounded like she was baiting me.

"I—I get that, but...going up against Nakamura three times..."

I shivered as I imagined it. I—I mean...I could just see him glaring at me and giving some retort that would tear me apart… This was not a guy I should be messing with…

"Well, you've got plenty of time, so make sure you choose the right moment. I don't think you'd lie to me, so you can do it when I'm not watching if you want."

"I—I understand."

I was happy to have her trust, but that feeling was rapidly disappearing under my terror of what was to come.

"Aside from that…this isn't even really an assignment, but…"

Hinami looked over at Takei, Mizusawa, and Mimimi setting up the canopy in the distance.

"It would be great if you could actively try to become better friends with Mizusawa."

"…With Mizusawa? As part of my goal to make male friends?"

Hinami nodded. "Mizusawa is currently your most likely candidate for a friend, and he'll also be the most beneficial in the future when it comes to conquering the game of life."

I smiled cynically at the words *most beneficial.* Hinami *would* think of it that way.

"You mean I can steal conversational skills from him, and he'll make it easier for me to join the Mizusawa-Nakamura group?"

Hinami nodded. It made sense that she was pushing this angle, given the fact that she'd already strong-armed me into a job at the same place where he worked.

"Yeah, that's the general idea. The closer you get with Mizusawa, the easier it will be for you to mess with Nakamura, too. Plus, you need to reach a point where no one will say you're hard to talk to."

Hinami sounded a little irritated. I wasn't totally sure why, but I had an idea. The character she'd developed herself wasn't getting the reviews she'd hoped for, and that was frustrating. After all, for her, this was practically a digital-pet game with me as the pet.

"Now that we've got that covered, let's get this fire started. It's not a glamorous job, but it's the most important one."

"Huh? Oh right."

For some reason, she seemed excited as she set what I think was a fire starter in the grill and piled charcoal around it. Her expression was focused, but I could tell she was having fun. Not necessarily about the barbecue itself, though—I think her gamer's spirit was on fire at the question of how she would clear the difficult and high-stakes puzzle of building a fire. Mizusawa called me weird, but I think this girl is way weirder than me.

She piled the charcoal like a chimney.

"W-wait, I don't think there's going to be enough pathways for the oxygen if you do it like that."

"Don't be stupid. If we leave the top open, an ascending current will form and create airflow."

"Really? But oxygen flow is so crucial..."

"I know that. Combustion is ultimately just a chemical reaction between carbon and oxygen."

"That's true. If you think about it, charcoal and air are the most basic form of combustion."

"Right. The primary component of charcoal is carbon. When the oxygen in the air reacts with that carbon, combustion occurs. And charcoal especially has lots of tiny holes for the air to flow through—another reason why it's the simplest, most effective, and most beautifully structured fuel."

"In that sense, the game of fire starting with charcoal is actually a very easy one once you figure out how to do it."

"Exactly."

"...So are you sure there are enough pathways for the air in that formation?"

"You're very persistent."

When we'd argued as we usually did up to this point, something occurred to me. I really had no right to get on a high horse talking about other people.

"Like I said before, this is perfect. An ascending current will form and draw air in from the base. Just watch."

"I will."

With that, Hinami's technique scored her a nice win in the game of fire starting. I had nothing more to say. *You've done it again, NO NAME.*

* * *

"...Nice. Got the pic. It's done!"

Takei cheerfully snapped a picture of the grilled meat with his phone before distributing it to the rest of us. Maybe this is a case of that "social media addiction" people like to say kids have.

"Yay, meat!!" Mimimi exclaimed. There was still plenty more on the grill. Every time a dribble of fat melted off the thick slices of marbled beef, the charcoal made a pleasant crackling sound. The onions, peppers, and corn had grill marks and gave off an appetizing aroma. I could hardly wait any longer.

"Hey, this onion looks weird. Who cut this?"

"Shut up and eat, Shuji!"

It was obvious from this little exchange that Izumi and Nakamura had a good time cutting up the vegetables together. Everyone aside from those two and Takei grinned, then dodged suspicion by complimenting the food instead or something. But seriously, the casual way Nakamura teased Izumi remined me of his top-tier status.

"Hey, Takei. You took the one I wanted."

"Wait, wait, wait, Shuji! That's mine!"

"You've been pigging out on the meat this whole time. Eat some veggies already."

"Aww, c'mon, Shuji. Yuzu, save me!"

"What?!" Izumi yelped. "Don't stress, Takei! You can handle this!"

"You're no help at all! Mimimi, save me!"

"Leave it to me! Hey, Nakamu, I don't see you eating any veggies, either!"

"Wow, Mimimi, bold words from someone who hasn't even touched the shrimp."

"Sorry, guys! I'll eat anything but shrimp!!"

"Okay, okay, I'll eat the shrimp and the meat for you," Hinami offered.

"The shrimp are all yours... Wait—are you after my meat, too?! By the way, why do you never gain weight, Aoi...?"

"My little secret ♥."

"Aoi loves to eat..."

"Takahiro, did you say something?"

And so the normie conversation unfolded. Watching them, I realized again how strong Nakamura was. One of his techniques was to store up little factoids like Mimimi's hatred for shrimp and deploy them in situations like this.

Comebacks were flying as everyone enjoyed themselves in the roasting heat. I'd never experienced a meal this wild before. This must be the true pleasure of barbecue. I'd always rejected this kind of vibe, but once I tried it out with an open mind, I realized it was actually pretty cool; the smiles and the sunshine and the heat of the charcoal all blended together into one dazzling scene.

Finally, the feast ended.

"Ugh, I ate too much..."

Izumi rubbed her stomach, her face a sickly shade of white. Nakamura watched with a frown.

"I warned you not to overdo it!"

"B-but...it was so good..."

"What kind of stupid excuse is that?"

"Sh-shut up!"

They seemed to be getting along great, which was the main goal. By all appearances, at least, our strategy to get them together was succeeding. On the other hand, my terror of messing with the all-powerful Nakamura was growing by the minute.

We broke into groups to get rid of the charcoal, break down the tent, clean the grill, and other stuff like that. Mimimi scolded Takei for slacking off in the middle to mess around on his phone. Apparently, he was posting pictures of the meat on Twitter. He was hopeless.

We finished cleaning up in twenty or thirty minutes and returned the rented equipment. It was time to launch our next strategy. This one was extremely simple. We were all going to hang out by the river.

We didn't know what to expect, so we couldn't make much of a plan, but since the two of them liked each other, something good would happen as long as we gave them the opportunity to hang out on their own. If the vegetable cutting was any indication, the outlook was promising.

"Okay, everything's been returned!" Mizusawa said as he and Takei came back. Surprisingly, he was wearing swim trunks. *Hey, wait, are you that serious about hanging out by the river? I didn't even bring anything to wear in the water.*

"Hey, hey, looks like Takahiro is getting serious! In that case, I'll follow his lead!"

Mimimi competitively pulled off her T-shirt and jeans. *Hey, now...* I couldn't tear my eyes away, but as it turned out, she was all suited up. Oh right, I guess she'd worn her swimsuit under her clothes. That was a surprise. I instinctively looked away from her flat, white stomach.

"Tomozaki, what are you looking at her like that for?! Gross!" Izumi teased.

"I-I'm not looking at anyone..."

My eyes turned involuntarily in Mimimi's direction again. She was wearing a blue patterned swimsuit, the kind with a sort of cloth that wraps around the hips. I already knew she had a nice figure from seeing her in clothes, but in a swimsuit, her slender waist and large chest completely knocked me out. Her legs and arms were long and slim but toned, with a faint tan that reminded you she was making the most of her youth. I didn't usually think about how pretty her face was because she was always so cheerful and her expression changed by the second, but during the brief moment of quiet, her doll-like features made a striking image with the summery scenery and the swimsuit she was wearing.

"Me, too!"

Hinami started pulling her clothes off, too. *So she was wearing her suit, too, huh?* She took off the T-shirt-like thing she was wearing but left her denim shorts on. Without her shirt on, she brought to mind the word *perfect*. She had the perfect amount of feminine fleshiness, but I could still see the outlines of muscles on her flat stomach. Her belly button was weirdly sexy. Her chest was really hot even though I think hers was smaller than Mimimi's—probably her posture. She was a hybrid of vibrant athleticism and feminine attractiveness. *Wait, what the hell am I talking about?*

"I wore my suit, too...but I think I'll just take off my shorts for now!" Izumi said.

She must have been feeling shy, because she slipped out of her shorts but left her T-shirt on. The clear outline of her obviously huge chest under her shirt together with the unusual combination of clothes on top but not on the bottom got my imagination working overtime. I'm sure she decided on that option because she was self-conscious, but the result was an even more erotic impression than if she had revealed more skin. *Argh, what the hell am I talking about? Someone* please *shut me up.*

I expected to end up watching the stuff by myself while everyone else swam, but it turned out that Nakamura and Takei hadn't brought their trunks, either. Okay, so I wasn't the only one who didn't immediately think *swimsuit* when I heard our plan of a barbecue followed by river time. At first, I'd thought I was just failing to keep up with the normies, as per usual, so it was a relief to know that wasn't the case.

But how were we going to get Nakamura and Izumi alone?

"So none of the guys except Takahiro brought their suits? I should have told you to bring them!" Mimimi laughed self-consciously.

"What are we, little kids?" Nakamura scoffed.

"No worries! We can still get in the water!"

Takei, who had been standing next to Nakamura, thrashed into the river fully clothed. It wasn't that deep, and he was wearing a T-shirt and shorts, but I was sure if he played around like that, he'd get soaked through to his boxers. *Wonder if he brought a change of clothes. Guess so, since we're spending the night.*

"Okay, guys, let's take our stuff up to the lockers first!"

We all followed Hinami's suggestion, then came back down to the river.

* * *

As I'd predicted, Takei was soaked through in minutes. He didn't seem to care, though, since he was splashing around with Mizusawa, Hinami, and Mimimi. Hinami's shorts (or should I say bottoms?) got wet, too, but knowing her, I figured she'd prepared for that.

I'm pretty sure the eyes of every guy on shore were glued to Mimimi and Hinami as they splashed around with girlish smiles among the water droplets glittering like jewels in the sunlight. A couple of guys in a nearby group of what looked like university students were watching them and whispering to each other. When the two of them got together, it was a real show.

Meanwhile, Nakamura, Izumi, and I were splashing around at the edge of the water. *Sorry, guys… You'll have to tolerate the trio since I didn't bring my trunks…*

Izumi kept splashing Nakamura, and she seemed to be having fun messing with him. He acted scornful but was still taking the bait. They were getting along super well, and I could tell how perfect they were for each other. *Better figure out how to slip away.*

For the moment, I focused on making myself invisible so they'd forget I was there. My long years as a bottom-tier character had helped me to hone this skill, so you could say I was in the perfect position. Everyone was probably already thinking, *Well, they're not alone, but it's just Tomozaki, so…*, and I had to meet their expectations. *Leave it to me!*

Unfortunately, the hopelessly dense Takei came over just then. "Hey, Yuzucchi! If you have your suit on, why don't you come out in the deep water with us?" *Man, just stay away.* The only people allowed over here are Izumi, Nakamura, and nearly transparent people.

"I don't want to get wet!"

"Oh, come on! Look, a little crab!"

Takei pulled his hand from behind his back and thrust it in front of Izumi's face. A little black crab was pinched between his fingers.

"Eek!" In her surprise, Izumi stumbled and slipped.

"Careful…!!"

Nakamura reacted in a flash. Kneeling down, he caught her like a knight carrying a princess. But even though he broke her fall, she still ended up in the water. Her T-shirt was soaked, and her hair got wet up to her ears. The ensuing splash got Nakamura fairly wet, too.

There they were, the beautiful girl and the handsome guy, dripping with water.

"Oh! Th-thank you…Shuji."

"…Are you okay?"

"Um, yeah… I'm not hurt."

"…Sheesh, don't fall over. Not cool."

"Shut up! …But thanks."

They looked very glamorous gazing at each other at close range with their hair and clothes all wet. Perfect setup for a kiss. *I guess if you want to keep your position at the top of the class, you have to remember to say, "Not cool," even when the moment's perfect? Better take some notes.*

"…S-sorry, Yuzu!! Are you okay? What's wrong with me?!!"

And then came Takei, who began apologizing profusely as he shook Izumi's shoulder. He seemed so regretful I half expected him to start crying at any moment. He totally destroyed the movie-perfect atmosphere, but he didn't seem to do it intentionally, so I forgave him. Based on his reaction, I could only guess that he hadn't considered how dangerous it would be to scare Izumi while she was standing in the river and had shown her the crab on a moment's impulse. Seriously, though, who has a sudden impulse to show someone a crab?

"Are you okay?" Hinami shouted from a distance. She must have guessed what had happened.

"I-I'm fine! Everything worked out!" Izumi stood back up with Nakamura's help and waved at Hinami.

Honestly speaking, Takei's behavior just now wasn't exactly the smartest or smoothest, but the end result was to bring Nakamura and Izumi even closer together than they'd been before… Oblivious idiots really are scary.

I glanced at Izumi. Her soaked T-shirt was clinging to her chest and stomach, outlining her body in unbelievable detail.

I could see the outline of her black swimsuit and even the color of her skin through the white fabric pasted to her form. The most suggestive part of it all was the way it clung to the two huge mounds on her chest, revealing every detail of their shape. The transparent, clingy fabric made

me feel like I was seeing something I shouldn't be seeing, something raw and sensational that affected my male sentiments even more than if I'd seen her bare skin. *Yup, Izumi definitely has big boobs.*

All the young guys in the vicinity were staring at her.

"...?!"

She must have felt all the stares, because she suddenly hid her chest with both arms. This had the ironic effect of pushing her boobs together and emphasizing their size. If I saw any more than this, I'd be in trouble. I turned in the other direction.

"Y-you should go change," I said. The image I'd just seen seemed to be permanently displayed in my head: The clingy, thin fabric. The two large swells. The translucent shade of her skin. Her flushed cheeks and moist eyes as she crossed her arms over her chest in embarrassment.

So a wet, see-through T-shirt was sexier than a swimsuit. Interesting. I'd just learned another important lesson in the game of life. *God, what the hell am I talking about?*

* * *

"That was so fun!"

Mimimi sounded thoroughly satisfied. She had changed from her swimsuit back into a T-shirt.

The sun was setting, and the sky outside was turning shades of pink.

"Yeah. I feel like a kid again!" Mizusawa said, nodding as he took his stuff out of the locker.

"Takei didn't just feel like one, he literally turned into one," Nakamura teased.

Takei promptly offered a pitiful apology. That was all it took to reaffirm Nakamura's superior status over Takei. I couldn't even imagine Takei teasing Nakamura. It was even harder for me to imagine myself doing it in the coming hours, but do it I must.

After Izumi fell in the water, she went to change right away and then came back to play around in the shallow area with Nakamura again. I poured all my energy into fading into the shadows, which earned me some approving glances from Mimimi. I'm happy that my lowly self could be of service.

"What should we do now? Head over to the cabins and chill for a while?"

"Sounds good!"

Our next plans efficiently fell into place thanks to Mizusawa's and Hinami's leadership. We would go drop off our stuff at the cabins where we'd be staying that night.

"Okay then, let's go."

With those words from Mizusawa, we split into guys and girls. Which meant that from this point on, I'd be on my own with Nakamura, Mizusawa, and Takei. Seriously? This was terrifying… Still, it could be a chance to complete my assignment.

The cabin was about the size of a large bedroom made of wood.

"Wow! Nothing in here!"

The cabin had nothing but a floor, windows, a door, and a ceiling—and that was apparently exciting to Takei. He buzzed around checking it out until he got bored and sat down. I envy a guy who can get excited over literally nothing.

"Think we can use those cards?" Nakamura asked, sitting down listlessly.

"Yeah, looks like we can borrow them for free," Mizusawa answered energetically.

"We're going to the hot spring later, right? Guess we'll kill some time till then… Hey, Tomozaki."

"What?"

"Hey," Mizusawa interrupted. "I've been wanting to ask you, how are things with Shimano-senpai lately?"

As soon as Nakamura said my name, Mizusawa changed the topic. I think Nakamura was about to make me bring him the cards. *You are one scary guy, Nakamura. B-but just you wait, I'm gonna mess with you!*

And this Shimano-senpai who Mizusawa had mentioned… *I remember that name! That time in home-ec class when Hinami told Nakamura, "That's why Shimano-senpai dumped you!"…Mizusawa must be talking about the same older girl at our school who broke up with Nakamura last semester. Nice one, Mizusawa. Gathering a little intel for the Izumi-Nakamura strategy.*

Information gathering is definitely crucial for beating a game. I always follow the top *Atafami* players on Twitter and 2channel threads to look for new info.

"...Why're you asking all of a sudden? Nothing's been going on whatsoever."

"Nothing?"

Mizusawa and Hinami are probably the only two people who could get away with pushing Nakamura that hard. I, on the other hand, have an internal rule that says, *Do not push Nakamura*, which is definitely a hierarchy thing. And today I had to overturn that rule three times.

"We talk on LINE sometimes."

"So you're talking again, huh? You trying to get back together or something?"

Mizusawa sat down next to Nakamura and started asking him all the questions everyone else wanted to but couldn't. Impressive. Would I ever be able to do this kind of thing? I listened to their conversation, waiting for my chance to get in a jab.

"She's with someone right now...but seriously, why'd you bring it up all of a sudden?"

"No real reason. Everyone talks about romance on an overnight trip, right?"

Mizusawa looked at me. I needed to help out however I could with the information gathering and imitate his aggressive questioning, at least on a surface level; I sat down across from the two of them and gave a thumbs-up.

"True that."

"Don't get carried away, Tomozaki."

Nakamura's superiority hit me hard. Damn, he was scary. And I'd done such a smooth job of answering! It was like he was really saying, *Someone like you has no right to answer smoothly.* He was too far above me in the pecking order.

Still, he sighed and mumbled, "It's complicated." The information was trickling out.

"Complicated how?" Mizusawa asked.

"She's dating someone, but she still texts me on LINE. She'll be like,

We're not getting along, like she wants my advice. I'm not trying to get back with her, but like I said, it's complicated."

"Hmm," Mizusawa said, frowning. "That is complicated."

"Basically, I want to move on, but it's hard."

"If you feel like you still have a chance with Shimano-senpai, it'd be hard to date someone else."

"And I mean, come on, look at her boobs."

The two of them laughed. Ooh, guy talk. Anyway, to summarize what Nakamura just said, it sounded like they'd been dating until she dumped him, and she'd recently started sending him messages about problems with her current boyfriend. Which made him feel like he had a chance with her again, so he was having trouble dating anyone else.

To me, that sounded like…

"What's that look for, Tomozaki?"

My thoughts must have shown on my face, because Nakamura glared at me.

"Oh, n-nothing."

"Ugh, why are you being so weird?" Nakamura was grumpy and merciless.

Mizusawa smiled at me. "Fumiya, you must have some thoughts on this situation."

"Uh, well…"

"What? Tell us!"

He looked at me, excited. What was he expecting? But I *had* had a hunch that now was the time to go after Nakamura. *O-okay, time to gather my courage…!* I took a breath and put my hunch into words.

"I-it's just, what Shimano-senpai is doing…"

"Yeah?"

"Isn't she stringing you along?"

The second I said it, Mizusawa burst out laughing. It spread to Takei next, and he started cracking up. I cautiously glanced in Nakamura's direction. He was scowling fiercely at me. *Y-yikes!* Of course, that was unavoidable. I'd just called him the benchwarmer equivalent of a boyfriend.

"You're pushing your luck," he said. But he didn't sound as intimidating as usual, and finally he seemed to give in.

"Yeah, I'm her backup," he groaned, shrugging hopelessly. Mizusawa and Takei laughed even harder. This seemed to be a pattern of his: Nakamura-being-laughed-at had turned into Nakamura-making-the-guys-laugh. Was that a technique related to messing with people and being messed with? If it was, it was way too advanced for me.

Anyway, my heart was pounding, but I'd safely cleared my first attack.

Finally, Mizusawa managed to catch his breath, wipe away his tears, and continue collecting information.

"Okay, that aside, do you have your eye on someone else?"

Nakamura clucked his tongue in a very revealing way, then answered with some resignation. "That's a tough one. There is someone, but she's asked me for advice about her romantic situation, too."

"...Seriously?" Mizusawa's tone changed. I jumped a little myself. If our assessment was right and he was interested in Izumi, that would mean Izumi had asked Nakamura for advice about another guy. What the hell? Izumi liked Nakamura, right? So did Nakamura like someone else? If so, we'd made a major miscalculation.

"What kind of advice?"

"She was like, 'I have a crush on someone, but I don't think they've noticed me. What do you think I should do?'"

"...Ah...hah..."

Sounding very concerned, Mizusawa pressed his hand to his mouth. Was it just my imagination, or was he trying to hold back laughter? Anyway, the story was getting very weird. If Nakamura was after Izumi, that meant Izumi had gone to him with that line about having a crush on someone— *Ohhhhh. I get it.*

My little aha moment gave me quite a shock. In other words, Izumi had asked her crush for advice on what to do about her crush! She was asking Nakamura for advice about Nakamura! No way! What bittersweet tactics! Suddenly, Mizusawa's laughter made sense.

"So your chances there are weak, too, huh?" Takei said innocently.

C'mon, are you okay? Even I figured this one out.

Still, I was a little surprised that Izumi had come up with such a solid plan. Or maybe this was typical for normies in their mysterious world.

My phone buzzed in my pocket. It was a message from Mizusawa to the Nakamura-Izumi strategy group Hinami had set up.

[*Apparently, Shimano-senpai's been telling Shuji she's having problems with her bf, ha-ha. That's keeping him from moving on*], it read.

When did he type that? I saw him messing with his phone, but I didn't notice him typing, even though he was right in front of me. Mimimi wrote back.

Mimimi: yeah, she does stuff like that
i don't like her!
Mizusawa: Yeah, she's bad news
Hinami: Is she stringing Shuji along? lol
Mizusawa: Fumiya said exactly that, right to his face. We freakin lost it

[*srsly? go tomozaki go!*] Mimimi wrote, along with a GIF of a rabbit cracking up. This conversation was on fire. So this is what group conversations were like? I'd better join in. I glanced at Nakamura and Takei to make sure they wouldn't think it was weird that I was on my phone, but both of them were on theirs. What the heck. In the turn-based battles of normie land, apparently there was a round devoted to phone time. Anyway, now was my chance. Incidentally, when I glanced at Takei, I saw he had Twitter pulled up on his phone. So predictable.

[*He was glaring so hard at me when I said it*], I wrote, and pressed SEND.

Mimimi: lolololol
Hinami: Tomozaki-kun is getting aggressive, I see.
Mizusawa: He's today's behind-the-scenes MVP

Wow, that message went over well. We were having a wild conversation, while being completely silent.

* * *

Hinami: Hey! We heard a bombshell from Yuzu, too!
Might as well try out a LINE comeback.

Me: Bombshell?

Hinami: Yeah. Yuzu said she actually told Shuji she has a crush on someone! LOL

Mizusawa sent a GIF of a pretty boy with his hand up saying, "Wait a second!" [*lol Shuji told us the girl he likes asked him for advice about her crush*]

Mimimi: oh shit lmao
they're totally into each other

Hinami: Get together already!

Meanwhile, as the four of us were having a party on LINE, Takei and Nakamura had formed a little club of their own and were getting excited about something else.

"We've gotta go soon. No other options."

"Yeah. Come on, Takahiro. You too, Tomozaki."

"What's this about?" Mizusawa said, standing up.

I hesitated, confused.

"Is that even a question?" Takei said, giving us a thumbs-up. "Breaking into the girls' cabin, obvs!"

I was pulled into the normie wave of excitement, and we all headed toward the cabin where the girls were resting.

* * *

"Hey, hey," Nakamura called, knocking on their door.

"What's up?" someone answered from inside, and an instant later, he barged right in.

"Bet you girls are bored," he said. "Let's do something." What was this power?

"I knew you would come over, Nakamu!" Mimimi said, sitting with her legs stretched out. I nervously followed Mizusawa and Takei into the cabin.

The three beautiful girls were sprawled casually on the floor among half-finished soda bottles and little bags of snacks. The outlets stuffed with chargers gave the room an oddly homey feeling, and there was an artificial smell in the air, maybe perfume or clothes, that was different from the guys' cabin. The odd combination of carelessness and girliness made me feel like I didn't really belong here.

"Something like what?" Izumi sounded slightly excited.

"How about a game? Like UNO or cards or something?"

A game. I wasn't the only one whose eyes glittered at that word.

"Sure. Which one should we do first?" Hinami's tone was smooth and gentle, but I could detect the competitive spirit underneath.

"How about Millionaire?"

"Okay! Millionaire it is!"

Hinami's cheerful announcement was the starting bell for a fight to the death.

* * *

"C-can you do that?"

Izumi was starting to sound scared. Since there were seven of us, we decided to play with three Commoners, a Grand Millionaire, a Millionaire, a Pauper, and an Extreme Pauper. Banishing had been outlawed, per Nakamura's claim that it was "boring."

As a result, we were now on round nine, and aside from the second and fourth rounds when someone aside from Hinami and I had been Millionaire, the two of us had been monopolizing the top two positions. I wouldn't expect anything less from NO NAME. She was really good, and I bet she'd probably practiced online.

Incidentally, we'd both been Grand Millionaire four times.

This was going to be our last round, and afterward we'd all go to the hot spring. In other words, whoever became Grand Millionaire this round would break the tie and become champion. I was determined not to lose.

I looked at the cards in my hand and thought over the best strategy.

Should I play a sequence...or keep back a pair?

If I played the sequence, I'd reduce my hand by four cards in a single turn. Since we weren't playing with sequence revolutions, the strength of the cards wouldn't be reversed, but I'd still be at a big advantage with four fewer cards. On the other hand, those four cards included half of three pairs, which was a major concern. Playing the sequence would mean losing three pairs. You were forced to play a pair fairly often, so losing cards I could play at those times would be a big hit.

In which case, I'd be conservative and play a pair now instead of the sequence.

A good decision as it turned out, because after that turn, I was able to quietly but steadily reduce my hand. When everyone else still had six or more cards left, I had two. A fairly strong position.

Plus, those two cards were an eight of hearts and a three of spades.

When my turn came around, if any single card lower than a seven was on top of the pile, I'd be able to play an eight ender and go out. Or if a revolution took place and three became the strongest card or if a joker was played, I could counter and go out that way. My preference was for a card lower than seven. I waited quietly for my opportunity.

But my opportunity didn't come. The problem was the seating order. Hinami was immediately before me.

Of course, I didn't expect her to casually play such a favorable card. But while I had two cards left, Hinami had six. With so many cards, it was highly likely that she'd have to play a weak single card at some point. That's why I'd held back my eight.

I watched vigilantly for my chance.

Several turns passed. Hinami cleared the old pile and started a new one on her turn.

This should be it. Since the pile was empty, she could play whatever card she wanted.

A standard move in this situation was to play a single weak card. By getting rid of a weak card that would be hard to discard in other situations, the player took a big step toward going out.

In the last round, Hinami had been Millionaire. Even though she'd passed one weak card to Mimimi, a Pauper, she could be expected to have one more weak card. And she hadn't yet played any single weak cards. In other words, the outlook was decent. If she played a single seven or lower now, I would win.

"All right, I think I'll..."

She paused, thinking over her move, and finally pulled several cards from her hand to place on the new pile.

Well, that was a surprise.

She'd played a pair made up of a five of hearts and a joker.

"Uh..."

The joker could turn into any card. If it was played by itself, it was practically the strongest card in the pack, and if it was played with an ace or a two, it made an extremely strong pair. Plus, if it was played with three or four of a kind, it could be used to cause a revolution. But she'd played it with a five of hearts, which had no advantage whatsoever...

I was surprised by her failure to obey common sense, but...I was also admiring how thorough her logic was.

She'd read me like a book.

She knew I had an eight in my hand.

My guess is that the five of hearts was a weak card in her hand, not part of any pair or sequence. She had to play it at some point, or she wouldn't be able to go out. It was a lousy inheritance. If the player after her was waiting for a chance to go out on an eight, like I was, she'd be setting them up perfectly.

That's why she'd decided to play that lousy inheritance together with a joker, forcing it into a pair. But a pair of fives was not strong at all. In fact, Izumi easily played a pair of nines on it.

In other words, she'd wasted her joker.

Everyone had looked confused when she played the five with the joker; it was a genuinely baffling move. Someone might even have called it a bad one.

But *I wasn't able to play my cards.*

In the game of Millionaire, there's no best move that works in all situations, aside from going out. What's important is to choose the tactics that match the situation. Hinami had just vividly demonstrated that principle.

Ultimately, she became Grand Millionaire without letting me play either of my cards. I went out right after she did. That meant she'd won five rounds, and I'd won four.

"No way! You're kidding!"

"Looks like I just won!" Hinami was grinning triumphantly at me.

"Aw…shit." I pouted dramatically, and I didn't even care that everyone was watching.

"What, you thought I wouldn't guess your hand?" Hinami was half playing her perfect-heroine role, half sneering at me with the tone she used in our meetings.

"Okay, you two. Why are you getting so competitive with each other? Millionaire isn't really that kind of game," Mizusawa scolded in a joking tone.

Hinami gave a fake giggle and pointed at Mizusawa. "At least I didn't lose!" she said.

"Can't argue with that!" Mizusawa said brightly, apparently satisfied.

Everyone laughed. As I was gazing at him in admiration, our eyes suddenly met. For some reason, he smiled in an almost lonely way, shifted his eyes away, and looked at his cards.

"Gotta hand it to people who take this stuff seriously," he said with a cynical smirk.

His words were almost lost among the meaningless chatter, but I couldn't get the sound out of my ears.

With that, the Millionaire tournament ended, and at Mizusawa's suggestion, we started to put away the cards and other stuff to get ready to head to the hot spring.

* * *

"How about you, Hiro? Anything going on lately?"

Izumi grinned as she squinted suspiciously at Mizusawa and poked him with her elbow.

"Oh, here and there…"

Nakamura peered into Mizusawa's face.

"Come on, dude? Aren't you going to tell 'em about the thing with Misaki-chan from Nishi High?"

"Hey, Shuji!"

"What?! Tell us, tell us!!" Mimimi squealed.

"Well, actually…"

Twenty or thirty minutes had passed since the Millionaire tournament ended. We had planned to go to the hot spring, but we'd started talking as we cleaned up the cards, and now the heated normie conversation was dragging on forever.

"R-really?!"

According to Nakamura, Mizusawa had been hitting on a girl at another school, and they were on the verge of dating.

Izumi latched on excitedly to this news. I'd already heard a bunch of girls at the karaoke place had a crush on him, too… He really was a lady-killer.

"I swear, it's true. Right, Takahiro?"

"Okay, I'll admit we're friends, but…"

"But you asked her out, right?"

"Yeah, but…"

"Yes! Confession recorded at six fifty-two PM!" Mimimi looked at an imaginary wristwatch as she jokingly noted the time.

"What? Well, if I'm going to confess…there's this girl I met at the West High culture festival last year, and lately we've been exchanging messages on LINE, so sometimes I ask her to do stuff on the weekends…"

"One-on-one, you mean?" Mimimi asked suggestively.

"Yeah, just the two of us."

"Second confession recorded at six forty-eight PM!"

"Mimimi, that's earlier than the last confession," Hinami retorted shrewdly.

Takei laughed loudly.

"Anyway! What did she say? Are you guys going to get together?!" Izumi leaned toward Mizusawa. She really liked this kind of gossip.

"Honestly speaking…yeah, seems that way."

"Ooh!"

"Yay!"

"Eeee!!"

Everyone erupted at once.

"But I'm still not sure what I'm gonna do."

"All he has to do is say he wants to get together, and it's a done deal," Nakamura said.

"Seriously?! Is she our age?! Older?! Younger?!" Izumi was practically insane with excitement.

"Older..."

"Older!"

"He likes the mature ladies!"

"Found yourself a cougar, huh?"

All this just because he said she was older than him? Of course, his smile wasn't completely cheerful.

"Come on, you guys! Leave me alone!" he shouted. Everyone laughed.

Finally, the conversation wrapped up, and everyone calmed down. Mizusawa stood up.

"I'm going to the bathroom."

I took that as my chance to say something I'd been holding in for a long time. It wasn't a topic I'd memorized or anything.

"M-me too."

...I had to pee. I stood up. I still didn't know when to go to the bathroom when I was hanging out in a group, so my bladder was about to explode. There was no way I could say I had to go unless I was tagging on with someone else. It hadn't occurred to me to go when I wasn't so desperate. Something to remember next time.

But anyway, becoming better friends with Mizusawa was one of my assignments, so I'd be killing two birds with one stone.

We left the cabin and headed for the bathrooms.

...Also, this was another classic normie behavior: going to the bathroom in a group!

* * *

The two of us walked through the dark campground together. The bathrooms were a couple minutes away in the camp center.

"Well, that sure was a conversation."

Mizusawa's tone was cheerful, but his smile had a bitter edge to it.

True enough, instead of going to the hot spring, we'd sat around talking that whole time. I hadn't managed to participate much, but I'd had an unexpected amount of fun just listening. I was surprising myself here. Maybe it was because I'd gotten to know everyone so well.

If you have time to get all mushy, then you have time to bring up a new topic with Mizusawa! I felt like I could hear Hinami scolding me. *Sorry, Hinami-in-my-brain. I will try harder.*

"Y-yeah."

As I cheerfully responded, I shifted my brain into gear. Might as well start with the cabin conversation.

"So you're into a girl from another school!"

"Ha-ha-ha! We're still talking about that?"

Same bitter smile. The dark woods around us swallowed up the sound of our footsteps and voices.

"No, it's just…I don't usually hear that kind of gossip at school…"

I remembered what Narita-san had asked me about Mizusawa, and I hadn't been able to come up with anything juicy at that moment. But now that I'd seen a little more of him, his true nature as a handsome player became clear.

"True, true. Some weird rumors about me and Hinami were going around there for a while, though."

For some reason, my heart jumped at that. I nodded. I could feel the sand crunching under my feet.

"But…are you really thinking of dating this other girl?" I was conscious of pushing along the conversation, but I was also just interested at this point.

"Huh? Not sure, actually. She's cute, and I like her personality, but…I don't know."

"…No?"

His answer didn't quite satisfy me. I thought he was the type to do things quickly and efficiently, so this was new. Guess even Mizusawa had uncertain moments when it came to love.

"Wonder what I should do." His smile was fake, and his casual tone was somehow distant. It was like he wasn't talking about himself any-more. Something didn't feel right, and I worked my brain for a reply.

"You think she'd be willing if you decided you wanted to be with her?"

"You mean what Shuji said?" Mizusawa gave a short laugh. "Yeah, guess so."

"Huh...wow."

Why was he so naturally confident? I wanted to shiver, thinking about how much of a natural advantage he had over me.

"What? There's nothing impressive about it. I'm just good at that stuff."

He was apparently being honest rather than hiding behind modesty. I couldn't read his expression in the dim light, though.

"...That's the amazing part. Here I am copying the way you talk and stuff, and this is as far as I've gotten. Asking a girl from another school to go out is way beyond me."

One of my few talents was playing myself down, and I used it to keep the conversation flowing smoothly.

"That so?" Mizusawa mumbled, looking down. After a minute, he continued.

"Yeah. Everything is easy for me. I don't even have to try."

I glanced at his face. There was something off about his expression.

He wasn't boasting or joking around. His tone was quiet and serious, even introspective.

"Th-that's, um..."

I wasn't sure if I should ask him about the odd look on his face. Before I could decide, he smiled and brushed over it in a joking tone.

"But even us winners can get lost when it comes to dating," he said.

"Huh..."

The conversation had moved on without me, and I'd missed my chance to ask about his expression a minute ago. Either way, he felt lost. About what, I wonder?

"You don't like her that much?"

"Ha-ha-ha... You don't beat around the bush, do you?"

"Oh, no, sorry."

"You don't need to apologize… That's how you are, Fumiya."

"Huh?"

Mizusawa pointed in front of him with his chin. "There it is."

"Oh right."

The camp center had come into view, and the cold fluorescent light was seeping through the automatic doors onto the damp dirt of the campground. Mizusawa took the lead going inside, with me following.

We stood next to each other at the urinals and peed.

Although it was night, a damp, warm breeze drifted in from the little window in a corner of the bathroom, along with the cool sound of pine tree crickets chirping. Only August and they were already out. Must be because we were in the mountains. Their quiet voices echoed gently in my ears.

"…Maybe I don't really like her."

"Huh?"

I turned toward Mizusawa. He was looking out the window at the slender crescent moon hanging in the night sky. Maybe it was the moonlight and the chirping crickets, but his profile struck me as faintly melancholy.

"What we were talking about before?" he said, shaking off the last few drops and zipping his fly.

"The girl at the other school?"

There was an unnatural silence as he washed his hands. Then he answered with more of his usual cheer.

"…Yep. That's the one."

So he didn't like her.

"But you asked her out, right? Just messing around?"

"I don't know. That doesn't necessarily mean I like her."

"Oh. Huh…really?" My comment was based on zero romantic experience.

"I mean, there's still a chance I'll date her."

Once again, I had no idea what was going on. "…Uh, um, what do you mean?"

Mizusawa laughed at my confusion, then asked me in return, "About what?"

"I mean…I don't really get what you're unsure about…"

"…Huh?"

"I'm not an expert on this stuff, but if you don't like her, seems to me you shouldn't date her, right…?"

Or maybe she was really coming after him, so he wasn't sure what to do? But he said he was the one who asked her out. Right?

Mizusawa looked surprised by my comment. Finally, he looked down and laughed, and I could tell he was hiding something. Then he looked out the window and scratched his head. "You're not just being polite, are you?" he mumbled.

"What?"

"Nothing! Let's get going! …You sure do take a long time to pee, dude."

"Oh, uh, gimme a sec."

I wanted to say it was because I'd waited so long, but I didn't. At long last, I finished up, washed my hands, and headed back to the cabins with Mizusawa.

That conversation was full of mysteries. Yeah. Everything felt unsettled. Guess some top-tier characters have problems that bottom-tier characters won't understand.

* * *

When we got back from the bathroom, everyone took a change of clothes and headed over to the hot spring a couple minutes' walk from the campground.

"Okay, guys, let's meet here after we're done!"

Hinami gave us instructions in the lounge before we headed off to the separate baths for men and women. There were showers at the campground, but since we'd come all the way out here and everyone loves the chance to sit in a big tub of hot water, we'd decided to go to the hot spring run by a different company. By the way, Takei had started complaining about how he didn't have anything to change into afterward. I guess the outfit he changed into after he got all wet at the river was his last one. He said he'd just put his current outfit back on. The guy is an idiot.

"Don't stay in there forever!" Nakamura said, slipping through the *noren* curtains hanging outside the guys' bath. Mizusawa, Takei, and I followed him. He never missed a chance for a casual jab. Maybe the hierarchy was built from a subconscious accumulation of these kinds of comments.

"Don't peek at us!"

"We can't!" Takei shot back playfully at Mimimi's joking voice behind us. I'm sure if he could, he would.

The four of us went into the changing room. I was insanely nervous. I put my wallet in a locker, found an empty basket, and...would now have to take off my clothes. Stripping down with three normies made me weirdly self-conscious. Terrified, to be more precise.

"What's taking you so long, dude?"

Nakamura was making fun of me. He was already fully naked. His towel wasn't even wrapped around his waist—he was carrying it. A force to be reckoned with. Even an amateur like me could tell he was extremely fit from soccer and general athleticism. I couldn't help comparing myself to him or the sorrow that ensued.

"Uh, sorry. I'm taking off my clothes now."

"What's with you?"

Withstanding Nakamura's suspicious gaze, I stripped down. My white skin and pudgy stomach were now exposed, the result of never exercising and spending all my time at home playing video games. Takei, who was already naked, pinched my stomach and laughed.

"Tomozaki, you look like an old geezer!"

"Lay off..."

Takei was at least as buff as Nakamura. His big shoulders and powerful aura were impressive. This guy was huge. After that second sad reminder, I stuffed my clothes into a basket.

"Not an old geezer...," Nakamura said, pinching my stomach. "A Moomin...no, a Fumin! You're in the Fumin clan!"

Takei started cackling. "Ah-ha-ha-ha! Oh yeah, he's definitely a Fumin. Turn this way!"

"Sh-shut up!"

I made an effort to sound cheery. Not just Takei and Mizusawa but even Nakamura joined in the laughter for once. That was a first.

"Hurry up, Fumin," Nakamura said as we headed into the bath. Takei cackled again. Oh man. I was the butt of the joke for all three of them. But when I thought about teasing them back, I had to admit I was the one with the saggy body, so there wasn't much I could do. Maybe this was essential training for the battlefield of tease or be teased.

Mizusawa patted my shoulder as if to say *Don't worry about it.* I glanced back at him. He was a little thinner than the others, but I could still see the shadows from his muscles. I finally understood the appeal of the legendary lean macho man.

I glanced at my own pathetic body in the mirror as I shuffled slowly toward the baths. Yup, no surprise they'd make fun of me.

* * *

"Hey, Takei, how about this bath?"

"Awesome!! Who'd guess a place like this had such a fancy bath?!"

Nakamura gave Takei a sidelong glance as he charged full force into the cold water. Mizusawa and I were washing our hair next to each other and talking about the Nakamura-Izumi strategy.

Meanwhile, Takei's screams ("It's so cold!!") were echoing off the walls.

"So, Fumiya—er, sorry, Fumin."

"You had it right the first time." Hinami had trained me well in this kind of comeback.

Mizusawa chuckled. "Anyway, the question is, how do we use the information we've gathered to get them together?"

"Yeah…"

I glanced at Nakamura, who was soaking in one of the hot baths. Thanks to Mizusawa's nice work, we had gleaned quite a bit of new information since we'd made the initial plans at my house. Based on that—well, no question about it, those two were perfect for each other.

"They definitely like each other, I think."

"Ha-ha-ha, that is the key point." Mizusawa laughed. We'd more or less known that to start with, but now it was an established fact.

"So now, if one of them would just admit it, they'd be dating."

"Exactly. Our job is to remove the obstacles and make it as easy as possible for them."

"Hmm..."

In other words, the goal of the trip wasn't to make them like each other; it was to take two people who already liked each other and give them a little push to take the next step. What kind of plan was that?

"Problem is, for those two, that's the hardest part."

As he scrubbed his hair, Mizusawa sniggered, and I could tell he was trying to hold back a louder laugh. He looked genuinely happy; I could see it in his eyes. He seemed like a different person than the Mizusawa I'd been seeing lately, who stared into the distance and sounded lonely when he laughed.

"Got any good ideas, Fumiya?"

I returned my attention to the strategy. I didn't have a plan...but I had a thought. "Well, I think the biggest obstacle in this situation is—"

"I agree," Mizusawa interrupted me, nodding.

""Shimano-senpai,"" we said at the same time.

"Yup. Her," Mizusawa said as he rinsed his hair.

"If she wasn't an option, Nakamura would probably go for Izumi, huh?"

"Ha-ha-ha, no question. She's leading him on."

"But we can't do anything about it."

Mizusawa frowned. "She's bad news," he muttered.

"Bad news?"

I remembered that he'd said the same thing on LINE, too.

Mizusawa made a joking face. "I mean, she's always going after younger guys. She acts all suggestive, so she's got tons of guys to choose from."

"Huh...?"

His unexpected answer puzzled me.

"Anyway, she's got good looks and a fun personality, so why shouldn't she play around with guys? And lots of them go right along with it. For half of them, it ends in a fling, and for the other half, they eventually develop feelings for her." His words sent a shiver down my spine.

"S-so, Nakamura..."

"Belongs to the latter half."

"Ohhh..."

I felt like I'd just heard something I shouldn't have.

"He was actually her boyfriend for a while, so it's hard to blame him."

"Huh, really?"

In a sense, that information reassured me. I wouldn't have wanted to hear that he'd had a little fling and then gotten overly serious about it. Even though it would make him easier to mess with.

"...Well, a bunch of rumors about her were going around even while they were together, but that's just part of her charm."

"S-seriously...?"

"Shitty, right?"

I felt my smile twitching. "In that case...shouldn't we just say that to Nakamura?"

"Okay, question for you."

"Huh?"

Mizusawa pushed his wet hair straight back from his face and smiled. He was handsome even with his hair sticking up.

"If we explained to Shuji that Shimano-senpai is a bitch who goes through men like tissues and he's only one of many in her stable of backups—do you think he'd let me tell him to forget her without a fight?"

I couldn't help laughing as I imagined Mizusawa explaining this to Nakamura.

"It would have the complete opposite effect."

Mizusawa smiled. "Right? He'd stop listening to me completely. That's why I'm waiting for him to realize the truth himself. He did laugh when you straight up told him she was stringing him along."

"Ah-ha-ha..."

"But that's the situation. It's a tough one."

Mizusawa stood up and walked over to the bath where Takei was doing push-ups in the shallow end and staying stuff like, "I could do this forever!" Mizusawa sat on top of him.

"Glubub! Pah! What the hell?!"

"Oh, sorry, sorry, you were going so fast I didn't see you."

"Seriously? This speed is dangerous, man!"

Takei was inexplicably pleased and started doing push-ups again. As I watched Nakamura and Mizusawa splash him in the face with water and push him under, I started to chicken out. There was no way I could keep up.

But Hinami had given me a mission.

I was supposed to mess with Nakamura and befriend Mizusawa.

I steeled my will, stood up, and got into the bath where the splash-Takei competition was going on. I walked right up to Takei with no plan whatsoever. As I was struggling to decide what to do, given that it didn't feel quite right in terms of the mood or my assignment for me to join in the splashing, Takei lifted his face out of the water and looked straight at my crotch.

"…Huh?" I was startled when I realized what he was doing.

"Dude, your dick is huge!!" He started to splash around.

"Seriously?"

"I wanna see!"

Nakamura and Mizusawa stared at my crotch, too, and yelped in surprise.

"Man, it's giant!"

"T-Tomozaki…!"

I could barely process anything anymore and sank down into the bath to hide, but it was too late. Mizusawa and Nakamura grabbed me, lifted me up, and examined the goods all over again.

"L-let me go!"

"This is crazy! It's as big as my forearm!!" Takei cried, and the other two started cracking up.

"Ha-ha-ha-ha! His forearm!" Mizusawa laughed.

"I'm changing Fumin to Forearm. Forearm boy. Farm Boy!"

Once again, Nakamura had given me a questionable nickname. Takei laughed loudly. *Come on, stop. Why do I have to get two new nicknames on a single trip to the hot spring?*

Still, among all the ruckus, I glimpsed a ray of light for my assignment. When he'd made fun of my body earlier, I was clearly inferior to him, so I couldn't return the jab.

Basic abilities and routine training seemed to play a key role in the tease-or-be-teased war. In those terms, how did my current prospects look?

I've never worried about average size or anything so I'm not sure, but based on his comments a minute ago, I might be bigger than him. Wouldn't that give me an opportunity to mess with him? If that was the rule, then maybe even a bottom-tier character like me could fight on equal terms or better in this particular ring.

Giving myself over to this thin ray of hope, I directed my gaze at Nakamura's crotch and confirmed my suspicion.

Oh yeah, I had a fighting chance here!

I focused on making my tone sound as teasing as possible.

"Wow, Nakamura, your dick is tiny!"

Nakamura grimaced, but Mizusawa and Takei clapped their hands and laughed. *Bam, two down!*

* * *

The four of us were in the lounge after getting out of the bath, drinking milk and joking around about various topics related to my nicknames and Nakamura's dick. Nakamura had been messing with me overtime since I'd made the comment, but I felt like his hostility had lightened. What was that about?

"Drinking your milk, I see!"

Mimimi was striding energetically out of the women's bath wearing shorts and a tank top, with a hand towel draped around her neck. She looked sporty, but with so much skin showing, it was inevitably sexy. Her cheeks were flushed and damp. I don't think she was wearing makeup, but she was so naturally pretty there was hardly a difference. I didn't normally think about it because she was so over-the-top cheerful, but she was incredibly gorgeous.

"I think I'll have one, too."

Hinami appeared from behind Mimimi. The first time I'd seen her without makeup, she'd softened her face so I didn't even recognize her, but

right now with her regular expression, she still looked like the charming, pretty heroine. Her flushed pink skin, which even I could tell was perfectly smooth and firm, had the power to ruin a man, no question.

"..."

Izumi came out of the women's baths behind Hinami, her face turned down. She was half hiding behind her hand towel; maybe she didn't want us to see her without her usual heavy makeup. But based on the glimpses I got, even though she looked a little different from what I was used to, she mostly just seemed a little younger. If you're good-looking to start with, you're gonna be cute even without makeup. Like the other two, she was flushed, but I don't think it was from being in the bath. I was having a hard time keeping my eyes away from her comfortable-looking short-shorts and long legs.

When I looked at the three of them standing there together, I realized I was on an overnight with girls of this level, and I felt kind of weird. I was way underleveled compared to everyone else here, including the guys. At the very least, I'd better stand up straight...

Ten or fifteen minutes had passed since we met up in the lounge and drank milk together. Takei homed in on the Ping-Pong table in the game room near the lounge, and we decided to play a few rounds.

Hinami arranged a doubles match between Nakamura and Izumi on one side and Takei and herself on the other, although Nakamura and Izumi barely needed any prompting to make a team together. The Takei-Hinami pair was the result of Takei's desperate pleading. The guy was out there enjoying his holiday exactly how he wanted to.

In the meantime, the rest of us could have a strategy meeting. With that in mind, Mizusawa, Mimimi, and I gathered around a small table in the lounge.

"We were talking about it in the guys' bath, and we think the issue is..."

"Shimano-senpai?" Mimimi realized where Mizusawa was going before he finished explaining.

"Exactly. You're making this easy."

"What can I say? She's a problem child." Mimimi smiled cynically.

"But if we point that out to Shuji, he'll dig in his heels. So we were trying to figure out what we can do on this trip."

"Hmm, good question!" Mimimi thought for a moment. "Think he'd be in denial even if we showed him proof?"

"Proof?" Mizusawa asked, intrigued.

"Well...," Mimimi said, taking out her phone. "How about this?"

The screen showed a Twitter account for Pretty Princess, with a bunch of replies: "I'm not getting along with my boyfriend right now" and "Cool, let's go to Daiba!" and "Sekitomo High! Heard of it?"

"Is that...Shimano-senpai's account?" I asked.

Mimimi nodded. "All these messages are to guys from Saitama who she met on Twitter."

"Damn. Seriously?" Mizusawa face-palmed. "So she's moved beyond our school..."

Mimimi smirked again. "This started out as a private account that only some of her female friends knew about. Guess she thought no one would find out, because she made it public recently, and now she's pulling this crap out in the open... All the girls are talking about it right now. If this is just the public replies, imagine what's going on in her DMs..."

Mimimi swiped the screen, and thumbnails of all the images she'd posted in the past came up. As she scrolled down, there were selfies of her face, pictures taken in a full-length mirror of her wearing a school uniform, of her lying in bed in the same short uniform skirt, her legs stretched out, a close-up of her cleavage titled "Look at my necklace," a close-up of her thighs titled "Look at my tan." Huh. Her profile was full of them.

"Th-this is...," I said in shock, "...way beyond what I expected..."

"Right?"

I understood now why she'd reacted so negatively when Shimano-senpai came up in the LINE group conversation.

"If we told Nakamu about this, don't you think he would cool off?" she said.

Mizusawa nodded, but he still looked skeptical.

"What, you still think it wouldn't work?"

"No, it's just—if you or me or Tomozaki told him about it, I think his lingering feelings would cool."

"And? Isn't that the point?"

"Yeah, but if he and Izumi ended up together during the test of courage after that…he wouldn't ask her out."

"Uh, really? Do you know what he's trying to say, Tomozaki?"

I said I didn't.

"Well, if he were to confess his feelings to Izumi right after he learned about the Twitter account, he could be accused of jumping into her arms on the rebound."

"Oh," Mimimi said, clearly convinced. "He's a proud guy, so you're saying he wouldn't do anything to make us think that!"

"Exactly. He doesn't like to be teased."

Once Mizusawa said that, I was convinced, too. It was related to the teasing involved in my assignment. For example, if Mizusawa told him about the account and Nakamura immediately confessed his feelings to Izumi, Mizusawa would probably give him hell. What's more, since I'd been messing with him during the trip, he might even worry that I'd tease him about it, too…leaving aside the question of whether what I'd done this far actually counted as messing with him, of course.

Since he occupied the top spot in the school hierarchy, Nakamura had to maintain a position that allowed him to give people crap without getting any in return. And in fact, I'd witnessed him many times messing with people at key moments and deflecting their attempts to push back—although I'm not sure if he was doing it consciously or unconsciously.

In other words, Nakamura was highly likely to avoid any situation that would make him vulnerable, like the current one.

At first glance, it looked like the stupidest kind of pride, but in the normie world—that is, within the value system of the school hierarchy—it was critically important. Through my assignments, I was gradually coming to understand that.

"Hmm, so maybe we shouldn't show him the Twitter account."

"Tough call. If we did tell him about it now, he'd probably make a move in the near future."

"Those two are so wishy-washy. You really think either one would make a move on their own?"

"Good point...and if they wait any longer, time will be slipping away..."

"But we don't really have any other strategy, so maybe telling him is the only choice."

"Could be."

They were thinking about the issue so seriously. They really did have good hearts.

I'd had the same thought at our first strategy meeting. Normies don't just think about themselves—a lot of them take the feelings of all members of their respective groups into consideration. Of course, that doesn't go for everyone, but maybe that serious consideration for other people is the reason they're popular and accepted—the reason they're normies in the first place.

I would never have realized that just by sitting alone in my room playing video games.

"It's gonna be tough to get things moving when we do the test of courage tonight."

Although Mizusawa was frowning, he seemed satisfied with that conclusion. Still, I felt like I should contribute. I thought about it for a minute and finally hit on something.

"Um..."

"...Aha!" Mimimi said, grinning at me. "Has the Brain had a flash of inspiration?!"

"Nothing that dramatic..."

"Come on, tell us!" Mimimi was looking at me full of eager anticipation. *S-stop it!*

"Well...you said Nakamura wouldn't feel able to act even if I was the one who showed him the account, right?"

"Yeah." Mizusawa nodded and looked at me searchingly.

"Okay, so right now Nakamura and Izumi like each other, and Shimano-senpai has already done plenty to make Nakamura stop liking her...which means all the conditions for clearing the challenge have been met. Now it's just a game of connecting them all together."

"True...but, dude, games again?"

"He's a gamer, Takahiro. Let him have this!!"

"Ha-ha-ha, true enough." Mizusawa nodded.

"Anyway, to sum it all up, I think the game consists of showing Nakamura the truth without hurting his pride…"

"Yeah, you could put it like that," Mizusawa said, nodding again. "But how?"

I paused for a second, not sure if I should go on. But I did.

"What if *we* weren't the ones who gave him the information…?"

"You mean have someone else show him?"

I nodded.

"Like who?!" Mimimi asked.

"Like…," I said hesitantly, glancing at the Ping-Pong table. "…Takei."

"Takei?" Mimimi sounded puzzled.

"We work it out so Takei tells him, and everything gets smoothed over."

That was all I said, and then I waited for their response.

"What would that—?"

"Ah-ha-ha-ha-ha!" Mizusawa's laugh drowned out Mimimi's question.

"…Uhhh?" I wasn't sure what he was thinking.

"No, you're right, that could work. If that idiot tells him he'll have no choice but to accept the truth." Mizusawa's gleeful cackling was reassuring.

"So…"

"I think it's worth a try! But there's no way he can act the part, so we have to trick him into doing it somehow."

"Trick Takei, too? What are you guys talking about?" Mimimi looked at the two of us blankly.

Mizusawa seemed happy to explain. "Basically, we figure out a way to make Takei realize that Shimano-senpai has been going after other guys and that she's dangerous. He'll think to himself, *Oh no! Shuji is being misled! I have to save him!* And then he'll go tell Shuji, because he doesn't know to keep his nose out of it. But if Takei is the one who tells him, Shuji will probably accept it, and as long as he thinks no one else knows, he should feel comfortable telling Izumi he likes her right afterward."

I was impressed by how perfectly Mizusawa had grasped my strategy. He may even have had a more refined understanding of it than I did.

Anyway, the point was that if the idiotic Takei—who seemed to stand outside the teasing hierarchy entirely—was the one to tell him, Nakamura would be able to humbly swallow the truth.

"Aha! I see!" Mimimi clapped, and Mizusawa grinned at me.

"Did I get that right, Fumiya?"

"...Uh, yeah." I felt embarrassed for a second, but I nodded.

"You sure did get a good read on Takei even though you haven't known him very long."

"I mean...hanging out with him all day today was more than enough..."

I'd had a front-row seat to his idiocy as he went around in his own little world—taking pictures on his phone, splashing around in the river in regular clothes, showing Izumi a crab and making her fall, apologizing profusely afterward, doing speed push-ups in the bath, discovering the size of my penis... Seriously, what was with that guy?

"So the issue is, how do we convey the information to Takei?" Mizusawa said, looking at me. "Do you have a plan for that?"

"Well..." I thought it over. "It's a Twitter account, right...?"

I explained my plan to them. When I finished, Mizusawa and Mimimi both gave their approval, and we filled Hinami in via LINE.

I was worried she might not look at her phone in time, but count on Hinami to have that covered. She noticed our message right away and threw us an amused smile. She'd probably caught on immediately.

All righty, then. With the help of Hinami, Mizusawa, and Mimimi, everything should work out. It was a mass gathering of top-tier characters, after all.

* * *

The strategy swung into action.

"Millionaire champions, unite!"

"Uh...yeah, let's show them who's boss!"

First, with Hinami's perfect performance and my monotone delivery of my lines, she and I formed a Ping-Pong team. Next, it was Mizusawa's turn.

"Hey, Izumi, you're on the badminton team, right?"

"Uh, yeah."

"Awesome. I'm sure you'll rock this racket sport, too."

"Oh, is that your point?!"

With that, Izumi and Mizusawa formed our opposing team. That left Nakamura, Takei, and Mimimi on the sidelines. Once everyone was in place, we started up our game.

"We were enemies in Millionaire...but yesterday's enemies are today's friends, as they say," Hinami said as she executed a save and smacked the ball onto Mizusawa and Izumi's side of the net.

"Nice, Aoi! This is gonna be intense...," Mizusawa said, wielding his paddle. "How about this?!"

He returned the ball powerfully.

"Oh shit... Got it!" I lobbed the ball back softly with a less-than-inspiring call.

"Yesss!"

Izumi was surprisingly athletic given how clumsy she was in ordinary life. She skillfully sent the ball flying back to us.

Meanwhile...

"Hey! Can you take a picture of us here at the hot spring?" Mimimi suggested, and unsurprisingly, Takei responded with enthusiasm.

"Okay, here I go! Hot spring!" he said randomly, snapping a selfie of the three of them.

As soon as he was done, Mimimi excused herself. "I'm gonna run to the bathroom!"

"Gotcha."

"Yup."

Nakamura and Takei started to listlessly scroll through their phones.

Back at the Ping-Pong table...

"Take that!" Izumi said.

"Oof," I replied. *Pathetic.*

The fierce battle continued, even as three of us were watching Takei out of the corners of our eyes.

"...Huh?"

I could hear him muttering something. Had he fallen into our trap?

He was silent for a moment, examining his phone with great concentration as he swiped the screen.

"Anyway..."

"Shit!"

Takei let out a little yelp at the same time Nakamura started to talk. We pretended to be so absorbed in our game that we didn't notice—except for Izumi, who was genuinely absorbed.

"What?"

"Shuji, look! Look at this!" Takei handed his phone to Nakamura, and a minute later, Nakamura reacted with shock, too.

"...What the fuck?"

I couldn't see what he was looking at, but I was pretty sure it was Shimano-senpai's Twitter account. Our attention divided between the Ping-Pong ball and the sidelines, we worked up an exciting-as-possible volley. Izumi was genuinely excited.

"She did this...?"

Now, I bet Nakamura was looking at Shimano-senpai's collection of sketchy close-ups and replies to various guys saying, "Yeah, let's hang out!" and stuff like that. His tone suggested a mixture of shock and liberation.

"...God, she makes me sick," he hissed.

"Sh-Shuji, I think you should forget about that girl..."

"...Yeah." He gave a humorless laugh. "But where'd you find this shit, man?"

"Uh... It popped up on my timeline... I think someone retweeted it."

"Who?"

Takei fiddled with his phone for a minute. "Huh? Where'd it go?"

"What the hell?" Nakamura sounded a little tired of Takei's antics but not aggressive. He was smiling.

Of course, Takei couldn't find the retweet. Because it didn't exist anymore.

The plan was extremely simple.

First, we lured Takei into opening his Twitter account.

Normies typically look at their phones whenever they have a free minute, but it's hard to predict what exactly they'll look at—could be LINE, could be Facebook, could be Instagram. But Takei almost always looked at Twitter.

So we had Mimimi go to the bathroom after a short conversation, therefore creating an opportunity for the two guys to look at their phones. But that alone wasn't a guarantee, so we added another twist.

We had Takei take a picture right before she went to the bathroom.

Takei had a high likelihood of opening up Twitter at any opportunity, but if he took a picture, his guaranteed next action was to post it there. We took advantage of that habit to ensure he would do what we wanted.

Next, Mimimi retweeted one of Shimano-senpai's infamous tweets with a photo attachment. Then, since Takei follows Mimimi and would be looking at Twitter at that moment, the photo would pop up on his timeline.

And since Mimimi had a private account, Shimano-senpai wouldn't get a notification on the retweet.

The key point here was for Mimimi to change the display name on her account. The way Twitter works is that when you retweet something, the original tweet shows up on people's timelines with a small note above saying who retweeted it. So normally, if Mimimi had retweeted Shimano-senpai's tweet, it would be displayed on Takei's timeline with a small note above saying "Mimimi Nanami retweeted," but no other information like icons or IDs.

Meaning as long as you change the display name, you can disguise who did the retweeting. Of course, if someone opens the tweet and clicks on the link that says "so-and-so retweeted," they'll go to your user page, so it's not possible to fully disguise your identity.

But honestly, how often do people look into who retweeted something? Or to be more specific, how often would *Takei*?

So we had Mimimi temporarily change her display name to the innocuous pseudonym Yu before retweeting Shimano-senpai's tweet. Then we secretly monitored Takei, and as soon as we detected signs he had seen it, we had Mimimi delete the retweet.

All trace that Mimimi was involved in this would be gone.

When she changed her username back, the miniature perfect crime was complete.

* * *

At Nakamura's instruction, Takei searched for the source of the retweet for a while, but eventually he pointed out there was something more important to think about.

"Either way, you should still forget about her, right?"

"...Yeah, guess so." Nakamura gave a vaguely forlorn nod.

"Hey, guys!" Mimimi returned just at that moment.

"Hey, Mimimi! You'll never guess what..."

"Takei." Nakamura shot a harsh word and glance at Takei before he could reveal all to Mimimi.

"Uh, oh...um. Nothing!"

"Ooh, what's the secret?!"

"Shut up. It's a guy thing."

"A guy thing?! Then it's hopeless...'cause I'm a girl..." Mimimi pretended to cry dramatically.

With that, Nakamura had sealed Takei's lips. Wonderful. All the pieces should now be in place. We'd communicated Shimano-senpai's true colors to Nakamura without injuring his pride, and he'd prevented Takei from sharing the information with anyone else. In other words, no one would be able to tease Nakamura over this.

By the way, nice performance, Mimimi. A bit too real, actually. Girls are scary.

We had just removed the last small obstacle standing between Nakamura and Izumi. Meanwhile...

"Ooh, nice one!" Mizusawa smashed the ball into our court.

"Ack!" Unable to respond in time, I let it fly off the table.

"Yes!"

"Nice one!"

Mizusawa and Izumi high-fived, and then Mizusawa gave me a meaningful look.

"...Looks like Fumiya is the winner of *this* game."

"Huh? ...Oh right."

It took me a second to realize he'd just complimented me on the success of my strategy. Hinami smiled and nodded, too. Izumi was the only one who looked confused.

* * *

Having finished both the Ping-Pong game and our big gambit without incident, we left the hot spring and wandered naturally toward the little woods nearby.

Needless to say, we were going to walk through the forest at night for our test of courage.

In a sense, this would be the final step of the Nakamura-Izumi strategy.

Even though the air was warm and damp, Izumi looked chilled. Her eyes were filled with pure fear, and she was shivering as she asked, "We're really doing this?"

"Of course we are! This is the main event!"

Ironically, even though we hadn't told Takei about the plan since he was so useless, his comment was close to the truth. This definitely was the main event.

"S-seriously…?"

Mizusawa patted Izumi on the back as her steps became smaller and smaller. "Don't worry, this is a normal road in the daytime. It's just dark and creepy right now. It only *feels* like a ghost could pop out when you least expect it."

"That's what's so scary!!" Izumi cried desperately. Mizusawa's clever teasing was extremely effective.

"Oh, here's where we start."

Ignoring Izumi's reaction, Mizusawa was looking down a dark, narrow path leading back to camp. There were two ways to get there—the one we'd taken on the way to the hot spring, which was a normal road that cars used, and this one, which was a paved but dimly lit path through the woods. The plan was to walk back to camp on this path in groups of two or three.

From what I could see, the path that veered off the main road was fairly dark, and honestly speaking, even I would have been afraid to walk down it alone. Not that I'm a scaredy-cat or anything.

"Listen…it's really dark down there." Izumi's voice was weak, and her eyes were pooling with tears. I saw her reach toward Nakamura and grab onto his sweatshirt.

Mizusawa's sharp eyes caught the movement, and he pointed to her hand. "Ooh, look at the lovebirds! Go on, you two; you first!"

"Yeah, I think she wants to go with you," Hinami said, piling on.

"Hey, no, wait! That's not what I…!" Izumi pulled her hand back from Nakamura's arm in a hurry.

"Too late. These guys have made up their minds. Let's go," Nakamura said. Sounding resigned to the fact that we'd never back down, he led Izumi toward the path.

"Hey, w-wait for me, Shuji!"

"Geez, keep up."

"Hey!!" Her voice echoed away as she vanished into the darkness.

"Nice one, Takahiro!!" Mimimi gave him a thumbs-up, grinning from ear to ear.

"Ha-ha-ha, what can I say? But it looks like…" He nodded several times. "Our strategizing ends here, huh?"

He was right. By waiting twenty minutes or so to send the next pair down the path, we'd give them some time alone at the campground, at which point it was up to Nakamura to finally make a move. That was the final stage of our plan.

"If we've set them up this well and Nakamu *still* doesn't do anything—C'mon, man up!" Mimimi snickered.

"Yuzu might be the one to make a move!"

"I hope you don't let that happen, Shuji! Think of your honor!"

Hinami and Mizusawa laughed along with her.

"Huh? What are you guys talking about?"

We all completely ignored Takei's question and started talking about who should go down the path next.

"Okay, I'm off!"

"Watch your step, Mimimi!"

"Aah!"

Mimimi and Mizusawa were the next to set off, twenty minutes or so after Izumi and Nakamura. We'd done rock-paper-scissors to decide on groups, and they ended up as the first pair. Hinami and Takei and I would leave after them. That was one unique trio.

"Actually, we planned it all out..."

"What?! Really?! Why didn't you tell me?"

"Come on, Takei, you know you can't act."

"Okay, I'll give you that, but..."

Since everything was over, Hinami was telling Takei about the true goal of the trip. He seemed crushed to learn he was the only one who didn't know.

Ten minutes or so had passed since Mizusawa and Mimimi had set off.

"Okay, guys, should we head out? ...S-sure is dark in here," Hinami said fearfully, and the three of us set off.

* * *

"Eek!"

Hinami freaked out as Takei stepped on a branch, snapping it in half with a loud crack.

"A little on edge, Aoi?" Takei leaned in toward Hinami, cackling happily.

"Sh-shut up, Takei! Scary stuff scares people sometimes, okay?!" she said sullenly, speeding up her pace.

"I'm not scared at all. Impressive, huh?" Takei crowed.

Hinami nodded. "It does make me feel safer to be with a guy who's not scared by stuff like this."

Takei smiled excitedly at Hinami's playful comment. This guy really was a simple creature. "Seriously? I make you feel safer?!"

"But...," Hinami said, looking at both of us. "Don't you think having three of us is part of it?"

Takei shook his head vigorously. "No way! Not at all!"

"So you could go by yourself?"

"Piece of cake!"

"Really?"

"Really! Would you be impressed if I did?"

"Totally. Only someone really cool and manly would do that."

"Seriously?! Okay, then!" he said, rolling up his sleeves. "Just watch me!"

"You're really gonna do it?!"

"Of course!" Takei strode confidently ahead of us.

"W-wow!" Hinami applauded softly.

"That's me! Ah-ha-ha!"

The two of us stood and watched him disappear down the path.

Um, what's going on? Hinami just tricked Takei into going ahead of us, right? So there we were alone on the dark path. Now I was a little…nervous.

"…What are you up to?" I asked quietly, my heart beating just a little faster than usual. Hinami gave me a satisfied nod.

"I figured it would be an efficient use of time to have a meeting right now. How's your assignment going?" She was back to her usual self.

"Oh…so that's what this is about."

She'd chased Takei off because he was in the way. I sighed at her cold, hard logic—my fault for letting my heart get excited.

"Hmm?" Hinami seemed to be enjoying my reaction. "What do you mean? What else could it be about?"

She brought her face right up to mine so her hair brushed my neck. Intentionally, I'm sure. *Ergh, okay…*

"N-nothing."

"Is that so?"

I felt my face growing hot. As I leaned back to avoid her attack, she gave a satisfied snort.

"What the hell?" I asked.

"We're going to do some special training right now." She wasn't even trying to hide her sadism now. I had a very bad feeling about this.

"Wh-what do you mean, 'special training'?"

"You know what I said to Takei, about being cool and manly?"

"Uh, yeah…"

"For example…" Suddenly, she shrieked and grabbed onto my arm.

"H-hey, what are you doing?!"

She looked up at me with watery eyes as I went into a panic.

"A-at times like this…you have to act manly and strong, right?"

Her voice was weak and feeble, somehow inspiring a desire to protect her, even though I knew she was making fun of me. I got her point.

"...You want me to practice walking in a manly and strong way with a frightened girl..."

My heart was pounding from the warmth of Hinami's palm on my bicep. She looked up at me with her frightened eyes and nodded.

"Yup, that's it... I'm counting on you, okay...?"

She wrapped both of her arms around my right arm and pressed herself against me.

"Uh, um..."

She looked so thoroughly frightened and vulnerable that if it weren't for the smile that briefly twitched at the edges of her lips, she would have had me fooled. I knew it was an act, but I still felt my heart beating faster. *I—I won't let you beat me, Hinami!*

* * *

Hinami walked along slowly, clinging to my arm, and pressed to me like glue.

"Ooh, it's so dark..."

"Y-yeah."

I was matching my pace to hers, my attention completely distracted by the very definite softness of her body all along my arm. Her chest... probably wasn't touching my arm, but her armpit and side definitely were. There was only a thin T-shirt between me and her bare skin.

"Eek!"

With a cute shriek, she squeezed my arm tighter against her soft body.

"C-come on...you're taking this too far."

I tried to take an objective approach to keep from losing my cool completely. Hinami, however, couldn't have cared less.

"Oh, Tomozaki-kun...," she said, bashfully looking into my eyes. "Don't let go..."

"...Uh, yeah."

The overwhelming power of the heroine was practically beating me into submission, and I found myself nodding. *Don't worry. I won't let you go*, I thought.

No, bad! What am I thinking? She had me wrapped around her finger. She was just trying to confuse me...but her face and expression and gestures were so adorable, and her body was so soft and warm, it didn't matter if it was all an act... And we were all alone on this dark path...

No.

Snap out of it!

I slapped my cheek lightly with my left hand to clear my head. I felt Hinami's finger tracing my ribs.

"Eee!" I yelped, and instantly my head was in a fog again.

"Tomozaki-kun...are you okay?" Hinami said in a concerned tone. *Hey, that was* your *fault!*

Anyway, I was supposed to be practicing my strong-and-manly act. She must be instructing me to focus on that.

"...Uh, yeah. I'm fine."

I made up my mind to just complete the special training and kept walking forward. After all, she was my teacher in life. Even if she did have sadistic motivations, I had to obey her.

As I walked along, my mind blurred by the totally abnormal and slightly risqué situation, a small insect flew in front of me.

"Oh!"

"Wh-what?!"

Overreacting to my small exclamation, Hinami let go of my arm and clung to me from behind. My brain turned to mush as I felt her soft body pressed against my back and her delicate, trembling arms around me.

I was done for. My brain was in panic mode.

"I-it's nothing. J-just a bug," I managed to say, albeit incredibly awkwardly.

"R-really...?"

She peeled herself off my back and reattached to my arm. I was disappointed that she hadn't stayed on my back a little longer, but I pushed down the regret and examined her expression. A satisfied smile was hovering around her mouth. *You're letting your true colors show, Hinami!*

But...shit. It was humiliating to be so completely at her mercy. I wondered if I could get her back somehow.

I looked around, feeling even more humiliated that I liked the weight of her head resting on my shoulder, and noticed a cicada on the ground in front of her.

There we go!

It was a risky bet, but if the thing was still alive...I could stomp loudly when we got close to it and sic the cicada on her. Since I knew what to expect, I should be able to control my own reaction.

I didn't want her guessing my plan, so I looked away from the insect and held my ground as she started making extremely girly comments, such as "Tomozaki-kun, your arm feels so strong and manly!" A few seconds later, we reached the cicada.

Boo!

I stomped loudly, and sure enough, it went flying into the air with a loud clicking sound.

"Eek, what's that?!"

"Whoa!"

Hinami's squeal this time wasn't quite so fake. *Ha-ha.* Aside from the fact that I was startled, too, my little scheme was a big success. *Serves you right, Hinami!* I looked at her with a self-satisfied smile. She glared at me for a second. *What?* Then she removed her arms from me and covered her mouth with one hand.

"Th-that was so scary...!" she whimpered theatrically, sinking to the ground.

"H-hey, Hinami..."

She looked up at me tearfully and shook her head weakly. "I—I can't stand up..."

What a faker. Bet this was her revenge for me giving her a little scare. Fine, then. I'd caught her off guard with the cicada, so I'd put up with it.

"A-are you okay?"

"I—I just can't..."

She looked up at me pleadingly. *Uh, so she wants me to...*

"You want me to lift you up?"

She gave a little nod. "...Uh-huh."

She lifted her arms slightly, so there was a gap beneath her armpits. *Okay, wait a second. There?* In a situation like this, wouldn't you normally pull someone up by their hands? But her gesture suggested she wanted me to wrap both arms around her and lift her up that way. *Seriously?*

"H-hurry…"

She looked on the verge of tears. I knew it was an act, but she still managed to make me feel like I had to rescue her before she started crying. *What the hell.*

"Uh, okay…" I did as she wanted, wrapping my arms around her under her armpits.

She put both her arms around my neck.

"…Huh?" I froze.

She gazed into my eyes.

"Wh-what?"

She kept staring at me silently, smiling and playing dumb. Her lips parted. Why was she acting so seductive?

But after my successful revenge with the cicada, a rebellious spirit had blossomed in my heart. I just stared right back at her.

She licked her lips.

Then she slowly pulled my face toward hers using the arm wrapped around my neck.

Okay, wait just a second. I stared at her with my useless determination to rebel. Was I going to keep putting up with this treatment? But if I looked away, she'd probably make fun of me for it later.

Through pure force of will, I managed to stay put. Very, very slowly, Hinami's face, her skin, her lips, moved straight toward me. The distance between us shrank from fifteen centimeters to ten and then to just a few. The faint, warm breath from her mouth caressed my lips.

Eventually, her nose was about to touch mine, and she tilted her head slightly out of the way. *Hey, people do that when—*

"Aah!!"

Unable to hold out any longer, I jerked my face away.

The next moment, I returned to my senses and realized what had happened… I'd lost.

I glanced at Hinami. She was standing there with her head still tilted and a victorious smile.

"Sh-shit...," I muttered. She was way beyond me. But then I realized something else. *Huh? Her lips...are where...*

"You have a long way to go, I see. Well, let's get out of here."

She stood up and I followed with a mumbled "Okay."

Her lips had ended up—exactly where mine had been a minute earlier.

...If I hadn't dodged, what would have happened?

...Had she been sure I would dodge?

My heart was beating like crazy once again, and the two of us made our way back to the campground.

* * *

The other five members of our group were already gathered near the camp center.

"Hey, slowpokes. I made it by myself, Aoi!" Takei called out.

"It wasn't that scary after all," Hinami said casually. She waved both hands, a blank look on her face. How was I supposed to interpret that?

"Oh, come on! It was super scary!" Izumi wasn't trying to put on a brave front, but now that a little time had passed, she seemed happy again.

"You were shivering like an idiot!" Nakamura commented.

"You don't have to call me an idiot!"

"Yeah, yeah, yeah."

"What's that supposed to mean?"

"Well, should we head back?"

Ignoring Izumi's question, Nakamura started walking toward the cabins.

"Wait for me!"

Izumi hurried to catch up so she could walk next to him. I'm not sure, and I might have been imagining things, but they seemed closer than before.

"Psst," Hinami whispered to Mizusawa. "What happened with Shuji and Yuzu? Did you hear anything?"

Mizusawa smiled like he was enjoying a private joke, and I listened in on their conversation as I walked next to Hinami.

"Apparently, he didn't tell her how he felt."

"What?" Hinami's shoulders slumped in disappointment.

"But..." Mizusawa smiled as he looked at Nakamura and Izumi. "They did make plans to hang out together."

He looked at Hinami, raised his eyebrows comically, and laughed.

"...That's all?" she asked.

"Yup, that's all," he said with the same silly expression.

Hinami sighed and gave a faintly tender smile. "Geez...I swear, those two..."

Mizusawa nodded. "Yeah...things move super slowly with those idiots."

His laughter was chagrined but happy, like he was watching with fatherly joy as an adorable little child took its first small step.

"I wish they'd take a page from your book—you got yourself an older girl in no time at all," Hinami joked.

Mizusawa shrugged. "Seriously. They're both good-looking and smart enough to talk if they wanted to. I just wish they'd be a little less awkward...you know?"

Despite his funny tone, Mizusawa's eyes seemed lonely and distant, even contemplative. He got that way sometimes, but I had no idea why.

"I hope things go well with you and that girl!" Hinami said.

"Ha-ha-ha, yeah. I hope it works out with her, too."

For some reason, he sounded like he was talking about someone else.

* * *

"So, nine?" Nakamura asked

"Yeah," Mizusawa said.

Takei had turned out the lights, and we were all setting our phone alarms and going to sleep...or not, as it turned out.

"Man, Izumi's wet T-shirt sure was sexy!"

Takei's excited comment set off a full review of the day's swimsuits.

"All she's got going for her is the curves," Nakamura said haughtily.

"You think so? I prefer someone like Mimimi," Mizusawa said.

"No way. Izumi's tits are the best," Takei said, continuing to push for Izumi.

"Hey, Farm Boy, you pretending to sleep?" Nakamura jeered.

Who's Farm Boy? Guess I have to go along with it.

"I'm not asleep."

"So what's your opinion?"

"I—I..."

Should I avoid saying the same things they'd already said?

"Hinami's posture...is pretty hot."

Nakamura burst out laughing. "I've never heard anyone having a thing for a girl's *posture*, dude!"

"Fumiya is a weird one."

"Farm Boy cracks me up!"

"I don't have a thing for posture...and stop calling me Farm Boy..."

As the raging wave of normie aggression washed toward me, my words tapered off weakly.

"Why? It suits you," Nakamura said meanly.

"True...," Mizusawa said, pausing for a beat. "They do say horses have big dicks."

"Ah-ha-ha-ha-ha!"

Takei cracked up. This was hazing...! Th-this was how guys joked around...? But in this ring...I could fight...!!

"Well...," I began quietly.

"What?" Nakamura snapped.

"No harm in being big. Better than being small like Nakamura."

Maybe because it was the second time I'd said something like that, Nakamura grinned combatively and took on a confident tone.

"Go ahead and say that, but I bet you've never used yours."

It was a flawless counter, and I couldn't reply.

"Uh..."

Mizusawa burst out laughing.

But even if Nakamura hit right back, that was number three! I'd completed my assignment! *Yesss!*

* * *

We joked around like that for another half hour or so, and then everyone started to get drowsy and grew steadily quieter. Finally calm, the three normies began looking at their phones. The light from the screens illuminated their faces faintly in the dark room. I took out my phone, too, and got to work gathering information related to *Atafami*. Not much later, a private LINE message arrived from Hinami.

[*You awake?*]

Wondering what this was about, I replied.

[*Yeah, what's up?*]

[*If you're going to be up for a while, I figured we could review your performance on the trip. You want to do it now?*]

Review my performance, huh? I guess it made sense. We'd still be here tomorrow, but today was the main event.

[*Sure, but what's the rush?*]

[*We could meet up afterward, too, but I thought this would be more efficient.*]

Logical as usual.

[*Okay, where?*]

[*Come to the front of the girls' cabin. We'll decide from there.*]

[*Gotcha.*]

I told the guys I was going to the bathroom and headed for the girls' cabin.

* * *

"There you are."

Hinami was a slim figure in the dark, her hair fluttering like silk in the night breeze. She sounded as cool as ever.

"Hey."

"How about we go to the camp center?" she said.

"...Huh? Oh, sure, we can sit down there, too."

We walked toward the center. When we got there, she asked me to give her a minute and disappeared into the girls' bathroom. She must have really had to go. We should've just met here. Oh well.

After a couple minutes, she returned. We sat on chairs in the lounge and started our meeting.

"I'll start with my overall assessment," she said.

"Please do."

"First, regarding your assignment to mess with or contradict Nakamura..."

I grinned. "I did it three times! The first time..."

I gave her a rundown of the "stringing along" incident, the "small dick" incident, and the "no harm in being big" incident. *Huh? Two out of three were dick jokes? Oh well, we're guys. What did she expect?*

"God, you're all dumb..." Hinami face-palmed. "But sounds like you completed the assignment. Pass."

"Yes!" I said, pumping my fist.

"I hope you understand now the important role teasing plays in multiple arenas: becoming a normie, making friends, and establishing equal relationships."

I nodded. "Relationships and hierarchies sure are scary..."

"Well, you have to kinda establish positions to make group interactions smoo—" Hinami broke off midsentence.

"What's wrong?"

"Wait, someone's coming."

The ice in her voice made me think maybe I should hide. I stood up and slipped into the little kitchen nearby. I heard Hinami saying I didn't have to hide, and then the automatic doors slid open. I peered out through the window in the kitchen door. Mizusawa was walking into the lounge.

"Takahiro? Did you come to use the bathroom, too?"

"...I thought you and Tomozaki were in here together... I must have been wrong."

"...Huh?"

Hinami played dumb, but I could tell she was on edge. Mizusawa went into the guys' bathroom and came right back out again. That was weird. What should we do?

"Huh. We must have just missed each other."

"Did you not have to use the bathroom?"

"No, it's just... Anyway, since we're both here, why don't we talk a little?"

He sat down next to Hinami. Uh-oh, was he staying for a while?

He sounded relaxed and loose, but the mood was awkward and tense.

First of all, I was curious why he suddenly wanted to talk to her. I also didn't understand why he'd said he thought Hinami and I were in here together, which was an oddly accurate guess. I kept stealing glances at them, but all I could do was sit there and sweat in terror.

"I wish those two would have made a move already."

Hinami introduced the topic searchingly, as if she were avoiding a definite conclusion.

"Yeah. I mean, just promising to hang out after we set them up so perfectly? They're beyond awkward." Mizusawa chuckled good-naturedly, but he had less energy than usual.

"Exactly! Just how naive can you get?"

"Right? Those two are awkward, naive idiots...no joke."

"Yeah."

Hinami sounded like her usual self. But Mizusawa was staring out through the automatic doors with that distant, lonely look in his eyes. As usual, I didn't know what was behind it. Finally, he went on talking.

"But at the same time...I'm impressed."

"...Huh?"

Hinami seemed mystified by Mizusawa's quietly mumbled words. Still staring out the doors, Mizusawa laced his hands over his head and stretched. He was keeping it light. Maybe he was trying to hide his embarrassment or avoid getting too serious.

"It's like... Okay, Yuzu and Shuji—and Fumiya, too, honestly—they do what they want. They listen to their own emotions. When they're happy, they're happy, and when they're sad, they're sad... They're always so sincere."

I jumped a little to hear him mention my name. But I remembered that he'd mentioned my "sincerity" and "effort" a couple of times before. And every time he mentioned those things, he had that same smile—that lonely, mystifying smile. In my head, I heard him mumbling introspectively, *Everything is easy for me. I don't even have to try.*

"…Yeah," Hinami murmured.

Mizusawa let his hands flop back down by his sides before continuing in that same light tone.

"Seriously, all Yuzu and Shuji have to do is make eye contact and they start blushing. Even though they like each other, they're so self-conscious together that nothing ever happens…and Fumiya, he's just so earnest about everything. Even if he screws up, he acts like he's having a blast…"

"…Shuji and Yuzu really are hopeless…" Hinami giggled and nodded. "But you think Tomozaki-kun is the same?"

"Yeah, Fumiya might be a little different…"

Mizusawa started laughing, too. "Yuzu and Shuji are idiots through and through," he said, repeating what he'd said to me before. "When I watch their little romance, and…when I'm with Fumiya, it makes me think about something."

"What's that?" Hinami asked sympathetically.

"I'd like to try being a little more of an idiot myself."

"…You would?"

Mizusawa nodded. "If I put it like Fumiya, every day is like a game, but I'm not really *playing*. I'm manipulating the controller, but it's like…I'm not the one moving through the world. Even if I mess up, it's the character I'm controlling who takes the hit, not me. And when things go well, I'm not the one who feels happy… I'm not the one having fun."

The joking tone Mizusawa had been using to hide his self-consciousness gradually faded into something more serious.

"…You mean it's like you're always watching yourself from a distance?" Hinami carefully broke down Mizusawa's explanation into something simple.

"Yeah, basically. So okay, the thing with the girl at the other school. I'm going through the motions because I know she's got everything you'd want in a girl, and dating her would probably be fun. I know what I have to do for it to work, but it has nothing to do with emotions or feeling shy or liking someone or disliking them or with what I really want."

Hinami nodded, chewing on her lip.

Mizusawa smiled with that same lonely look in his eyes.

* * *

"All I'm doing is putting on a good performance."

Mizusawa's small, earnest words echoed across the large, empty room.

"Hmm," Hinami said, looking him in the eye as she listened. The only sounds in the quiet room were their two voices and the soft hum of the vending machine glowing in the corner.

Should I be overhearing all this? The guy with everything, the top-tier character who could do anything, the one who was so perfect I used him as a model for my own attempts to become a normie—he was showing his vulnerable side, his true feelings. I think he was revealing his sense of inferiority and regret for not pouring his true self into anything. Was it okay for me to be eavesdropping on that conversation?

I tensed my legs.

Mizusawa sighed softly. "...Anyway, I just don't know," he said.

"Know what?"

Mizusawa looked straight at Hinami. She didn't look away.

They were silent for a second, their eyes locked and utterly serious. Finally, Mizusawa spoke. It was like he was tearing through the tension with his fingernails.

"Isn't it the same for you?"

I gasped. My whole body was tense now.

He'd just leveled a quiet accusation at her. He'd looked into the face of the perfect heroine—that face that fooled everyone—and realized that it was a mask born from a perfectly calculated performance.

I'm not sure if it was fake or real, but Hinami glanced around the room like she was at a loss for what to say.

"You're asking if I'm watching myself from a distance, too?"

"Yeah."

Mizusawa nodded. I knew the real Hinami, and he'd hit the bull's-eye with his guess.

To play the part of the perfect heroine, to reign from the top in our school hierarchy, in athletics, and in academics, she wore a mask made of blood, sweat, and tears. There was no question that mask was there with her perfect, brilliant smile.

The mood grew tense and still once again.

Mizusawa didn't try to escape the awkwardness with one of his embarrassed smiles. He simply gazed deeply into Hinami's eyes, utterly sincere. She grinned back at him.

"You could be right."

And she confirmed his guess.

The look she gave him was equally earnest, and he didn't look away. I couldn't turn away, either.

"Yeah…that's what I thought." Mizusawa smiled and looked down. Hinami nodded, still watching him, and spoke again.

"I…"

I was so focused on her voice, it was like my mind wasn't my own anymore.

"…I'm gonna be totally honest here. People expect so much from me, right? They're like, 'Aoi Hinami is good at everything!'"

But the words that came out of her mouth—

"I unconsciously suppress my real self… Honestly speaking, it's more like I'm playing the part everyone wants me to play, instead of doing what I really want. I feel like I have to live up to their expectations, so I work really hard. And of course, the more I achieve, the less I want to disappoint people! I'm just too proud, I guess. Oh, but don't tell anyone!"

—They weren't the words of the unmasked Aoi Hinami I knew.

"So I think I might understand how you feel. When you never do what you want and never listen to your emotions… When you just do what you think you're supposed to do, it always gets boring. That…happens to me, too."

—They weren't her usual rational, coldly logical, painfully truthful words.

"But I don't think there's anything you can do about it. People like Shuji and Yuzu are unusual. They've got so much going for them, right? And they're idiots! And Tomozaki-kun is a weird one, too. Ah-ha-ha. That stuff is impossible for normal people! I think all normal people…are acting a little bit. I think…you need to find at least one person you can show your real self to, as a kind of compromise, right? That's just how I see it, of course!"

—It was a flimsy, casual confession from the mask of the perfect heroine.

I was dumbfounded.

I mean, this was Aoi Hinami.

The truth was, the person she showed to everyone on a daily basis was a mask, a created character she was controlling through a never-ending video game. Without waiting for her permission, Mizusawa had suddenly crashed straight into that truth. But she couldn't have cared less for his attempt at honesty. She was like the final boss kicking aside an NPC; without even breaking a sweat, she had magically transformed truth into fiction and performed a perfect role-play of the school heroine earnestly responding to a classmate who had opened up to her.

I couldn't hear a single trace of NO NAME in the words she had just spoken.

"…Ha-ha-ha."

There was no humor in Mizusawa's laugh.

"Wh-what?" Hinami said, making her voice sound confused.

"You're truly incredible, Aoi."

"Huh? I didn't say anything that—"

"You can stop now."

Mizusawa's serious tone shut Hinami up. But that, too, seemed like part of her performance. As he stood before that overpowering final boss, Mizusawa smiled belligerently, like he was enjoying the fight.

"Strange, isn't it? Usually, I'm the one who's playing the perfect guy for whatever girl I'm talking to. I'm the one drawing out her real feelings, listening kindly, and wrapping her around my little finger the whole time."

To me, Mizusawa looked excited by the current situation.

"...I just showed you the real me, but you're still acting. Isn't it supposed to work the other way around? This has never happened to me before!" He cackled with genuine amusement.

"H-huh? What are you talking about...?" Hinami made a perplexed perfect heroine face.

"You're the only one I can't beat." He was admitting defeat, but he sounded oddly satisfied.

"Is that a compliment?" Hinami's joke was delivered with a perfectly light, teasing tone.

"Listen. I've been open with you, so I might as well tell you one more thing."

"Huh? Wh-what?"

Mizusawa grinned, his eyes glittering.

"I think I like you. I'd like to talk to the real you sometime."

Hinami made a fairly surprised expression at that. Then she mumbled, "Thanks."

"But even if I asked you out, you'd say no, wouldn't you?"

"...I'm sorry," Hinami murmured, looking down.

Mizusawa laughed cheerfully. "Ha-ha-ha. I mean, if you won't open up even after all that, there's no way we can date."

"I'm sorry."

Her second apology seemed like an attempt to evade the real meaning of his words.

Mizusawa nodded, still smiling. "Yeah, it does sting a little. Opening up and getting shot down."

"...Yeah."

Mizusawa's eyes looked sad and anxious, but at the same time, a satisfied expression played around his mouth. "But...," he said, stretching both hands toward the ceiling and smiling as if the storm had passed. "Sure does feel good to get it off my chest!" With a boyish, friendly expression, he chuckled. I'd never seen him laugh at himself that way. "Man, it's been a long time since I asked myself what I wanted and really gave it a shot." He scratched his neck.

"Ah-ha-ha. So you like me that much, huh?" Hinami continued her perfect performance, this time playing the girl who said the right thing to smooth over the awkwardness after she'd turned down a guy.

"I'm gonna tell you something, though. Now that I've bared my soul, I don't intend to give up." He sounded deadly serious.

"Is that so? I'm a formidable opponent, you know." Hinami added a silly smile to her joking tone, but Mizusawa didn't crack the slightest smile. He just looked at her once more.

"Hey, Aoi."

"...Yeah?"

He was advancing on the final-boss-level monster Aoi Hinami head-on. "Tell me something."

"...What?"

He was talking straight to the Aoi Hinami behind the mask.

"How long are you gonna be on that side?"

His eyes were focused very intently and very earnestly on her.

* * *

Once again, the only sound in the quiet room was the soft hum of the glowing vending machine. Everything felt weird. I kept my breath quiet as I thought things over, then finally arrived at a conclusion. In the shadow of the kitchen door, I got ready to stand—and burst out of hiding.

"—I-I'm sorry! I didn't mean for this to happen!" I flew out of the little kitchen.

"...Fumiya?" Mizusawa looked at me in surprise.

Out of his view, Hinami slapped her forehead in exasperation.

"I—I thought you'd get suspicious if you saw me here with Hinami, so I hid, but I didn't think it would end up like this... I'm so sorry!"

I was working my brain to explain myself as fully as possible.

Hinami followed suit. "What happened was, we bumped into each other coming out of the bathroom. We'd been talking for a little while when you showed up, and Tomozaki-kun went and hid for some reason, and then he didn't come back out."

Mizusawa sighed lifelessly. "Damn, you really overheard some weird stuff."

"I-I'm so sorry…" I really did regret what had happened.

"But I don't think you meant any harm… I mean, who would jump out and admit everything now of all times?" He laughed cheerfully.

"W-well…ha-ha-ha." I followed his lead and laughed, too.

"Seriously, man, only an idiot is *that* honest." He sounded a little fed up.

"I-it's just… I thought…it wasn't a good idea to keep hiding…"

Mizusawa smiled as I stumbled through an explanation and then mumbled, "Figures."

"Huh?"

Suddenly, Hinami clapped once. "Okay, let's pretend none of this ever happened and get back to our cabins!"

"…Yeah. Come on, Fumiya."

"Oh right."

Still flustered, I followed along. We walked Hinami back to her cabin and then headed to our own.

"…I don't intend to pretend none of that ever happened," Mizusawa murmured after her as she headed into the girls' cabin.

I'm not sure if Hinami heard him or not.

The next day as we headed back on the bus, Nakamura and Izumi were chatting as compatibly as ever, and Hinami and Mizusawa were making conversation with everyone as cheerfully as ever. I felt like laughing at how little had changed. But to me, even if Nakamura and Izumi were more or less the same after their test of courage, the lack of change in Hinami was something different altogether.

4

A single choice can change everything

It was the night after I got home from the barbecue trip, and I was lying on my bed thinking about a whole bunch of stuff. My thoughts were completely scattered. I couldn't get the conversation between Mizusawa and Hinami out of my mind. Of course, it had been a shock to witness Mizusawa tell her he liked her...but something else stuck with me even more.

Mizusawa had come to a decision on the trip.

He'd resolved to throw away his mask and go for what he really wanted in life.

Hinami had seen him make that choice, yet she hadn't budged an inch from her own chosen path—fiercely protecting her mask and delivering a flawless performance.

The two of them seemed similar in some ways, and yet at their core, they were fundamentally different.

The mask and the truth, the performance and the real self, the player and the character—their paths diverged according to which side of each dichotomy they valued more.

To choose the mask or the truth.

To continue the performance or to become their real self.

To view reality as a player or a character.

Weren't the choices they had made deeply connected to my own situation right now?

I was wrestling with an uncomfortable hunch.

Aoi Hinami, who was always right, didn't have the answer this time.

The answer was in *those words* that kept replaying in the back of my mind.

At least, I had a hunch that's where the answer was.

And then there was the LINE message Hinami had sent me a couple minutes earlier.

[*At the end of the fireworks, tell Kikuchi-san how you feel about her.*]

I didn't know how to react to that assignment. When I asked her for more info, she said that from what I'd told her about our last date, my chances of success looked high. Plus, the special setting of the fireworks would boost my chances even more. Finally, even if Kikuchi-san rejected me, it would be good experience that I could apply in the future.

Her words were convincing, and I knew what she was saying was probably right and that doing what she said would be the most efficient choice.

But I felt like she was telling me to just put on a good performance. It felt wrong—repulsive. What should I do? I felt like I'd been hurled straight into impenetrable darkness.

The fireworks were coming up the following night.

* * *

It was six thirty PM. The summer sun was low in the sky, on the cusp between evening and night. The plaza in front of Toda Koen Station was packed with people. They were everywhere I looked. No matter where I went, I'd be breathing in the air someone else had just exhaled, and I instinctively started taking shallower breaths. It was amazing that the fireworks had attracted such a huge crowd.

I figured it would be hard to find Kikuchi-san among all those people, but I shouldn't have worried. Her magical powers had grown twentyfold, so it was impossible to miss her.

I peered around the road running in front of the station, drawing ever nearer to the source of the magical power.

"Kikuchi-san."

"Oh! ...Tomozaki-kun."

As soon as she spotted me, her anxious expression transformed into a peaceful one. That alone was almost enough to do me in. But there was more.

"...A yukata."

"Oh...yes." Kikuchi-san looked down modestly and stepped back a few paces, I guess from shyness. Her geta sandals clacked against the pavement. "I—I thought I'd go ahead and wear it..."

"Oh, um, yeah."

She glanced up at me, and our eyes met. "...Since it's a special occasion."

"...Oh, uh-huh."

Her brief explanation delivered the finishing blow. Luckily, the moment before I toppled over, I managed to chug some of my bottled tea, which saved my sanity in the nick of time, even if my ability to think was still in shambles.

"Th-there are so many people."

"...Yeah."

"...Should we get going?"

"...Okay."

We headed toward Todabashi Bridge, where the fireworks would take place. We were walking a little closer than usual to make sure we wouldn't get separated.

Now that I had a chance to look more closely, I saw Kikuchi-san was wearing an indigo-blue cotton kimono with a Japanese pattern on it, accented by a yellow sash. I think the reason she looked so elegant and refined despite the less-subdued color combination was her natural aura and magical energy like a clear stream of water.

As I looked for the right road, my heart felt at risk of giving in completely to the overwhelming sense of summer enchantment emanating from Kikuchi-san. Each clack of her geta was reverberating evocatively through my head. I'd slacked on figuring out a route ahead of time because I'd assumed we could follow the huge crowd of people all going to the same place, but the throng of people split in several directions outside the station. *Uh-oh.*

"Do you think everyone is headed for the fireworks?"

"I'm…guessing so."

Could I assume people were going different ways to avoid overcrowding any one route, since all roads led to the viewing area? To be safe, I chose the street with the most people. As they say, the king's road is the right road.

"Should we try going this way?" I suggested.

"Um, okay."

Kikuchi-san nodded and followed alongside me with delicate steps. Her steps were a little shorter than usual, maybe because of the geta, but she made a perfect picture walking along so elegantly. The Japanese-print yukata set off her petite shoulders and glowing white skin. My usual impression of her was as a fairy from a fantasy story, so I'd assumed she looked best in Western-style clothes like the maid uniform from the café where she worked. Seeing her in a kimono felt like a new discovery. Basically, she was a fairy-slash-angel-slash-elf no matter what she wore. I couldn't stop looking at her.

Suddenly, our eyes met.

"Uh, um…Tomozaki-kun."

"…Huh?"

Suddenly coming back to earth, I saw that Kikuchi-san was looking down shyly.

"…I get embarrassed…when people look at me too much…"

"Oh! Uh, um…I-I'm sorry… I didn't mean…"

"Oh, uh, I know you didn't mean…anything, but…um…"

"Oh right…um, sorry, I…"

"Uh, it's fine…"

The red of her cheeks joined the dark blue and yellow of her yukata, making her into an even more beautiful fairy than before.

After a while, we came to a part of the street lined with festival stalls.

"Oh…look!" She'd spotted the candy apples.

"D-do you want one?"

"…Mm-hmm."

Her geta clacking sonorously, she walked over to the stall and asked for an apple. But before I could follow her over to pay, I was stopped in my tracks by the sight of her holding it. She was so beautiful I thought I might actually faint.

A minute or two passed.

"...I bought it," she said, walking toward me. Her usual soft, light, fairylike appearance was married with the eye-catching yet grounded elegance of the yukata. And to top it all off, she was holding the round bright-red fruit.

She was perfect.

"...Uh, okay," I said, staring at her again. "Sh-should we go?"

Focusing single-mindedly on keeping my cool, I barely managed to lead the way down the street.

* * *

"Wow, there sure are lots of people here."

"Yes, it's quite the crowd!"

We'd arrived at the banks of the Arakawa River and were looking for a place to sit. The show was scheduled to start in about ten minutes, and most of the free seating was already taken, so we were searching for any little gap. The whole shore was packed with people, with barely a crevice between the plastic sheets that were laid out to sit on.

Kikuchi-san seemed to find the scene delightfully novel. *Makes sense.* I guess for someone who descended so recently from the heavens, the worldly customs of human beings must seem refreshing.

"I think I see a spot over there!"

"Oh, you're right!"

After circling the whole area, we found a spot just big enough for the two of us between two large groups. I spread out the plastic sheet Hinami had instructed me to bring, and we sat down.

"Oh...Tomozaki-kun, thank you very much...," she said, lowering her lashes.

"Um, um, it's nothing..."

Kikuchi-san sat down elegantly on the sheet.

According to Hinami, "There are good spots and bad spots, but basically wherever you sit, it'll be beautiful." And if Hinami says so, it's probably true.

"It's been ages since I went to see fireworks," Kikuchi-san said.

"Really? Same here… I guess I haven't been since I used to go with my family."

"Yes! …Me neither!"

The conversation ended.

On this day, I was doing something different from our movie date. This whole time, I hadn't brought up a single one of my memorized topics. More to the point, I didn't memorize any for today. Naturally, there were more silences than when we went to the movie. But that was my strategy for testing out the truth of *those words.*

"Oh, it's starting!"

A small starburst lit up the crowd, announcing the start of the show. A few seconds later, there was a loud boom.

"Oh, it's starting…"

Another small one went off. Kikuchi-san's upturned face was tinted yellow.

According to some info I'd looked up online before we came, the Todabashi fireworks happen on the same day and time as the Itabashi fireworks, and you can see the other show in the distance from either location. Both shows are fairly large on their own, and if you add up the number of fireworks from both, they can rival the largest firework shows in Tokyo. In other words, even though they're a good distance apart, the show is actually fairly major.

The crowd around us was buzzing pleasantly. It wasn't hushed exactly, but for such a large gathering of people, I felt like it was impressively quiet. Most people were gazing casually at the sky, but others were looking at their phones or chatting with friends or peering down at the yakisoba they'd bought at one of the stalls. Everyone was doing their own thing. Big crowds are like that—somehow lively, considerate, and quiet all at once.

* * *

The colorful fireworks blossomed in the dark sky.

The delicate bursts of red, blue, green, and pink overlapped one another, sharing the sky to create a single magical fantasy. They radiated outward, drifted down to earth in a trail of white afterimages, and faded. The glittering magic seemed to fill the entire sky. There were wonders small and big, powerful explosions, and the exquisite beauty made by all of them together.

Before I knew it, I was completely drawn in. Kikuchi-san seemed to be, too.

"Wow..."

"...Yeah."

"It's so beautiful, isn't it...?"

The colors of the summer night lit up Kikuchi-san's face as she gazed spellbound at the fireworks.

"Yes, it's beautiful."

Sitting there on the dim riverbank, warm from the lingering heat of the afternoon sun and the crowds of people, her face lit by the magical glow, Kikuchi-san looked incredibly beautiful and sacred and serene to me. Time flowed by us in a quiet, sparkling stream.

I sat wordlessly, not searching for something to say but simply drinking in the sensations around me and enjoying the moment. If words arose naturally, I said them. That was my guiding principle for the night.

"Um..."

I had been wondering about something. Kikuchi-san looked up at me.

"...Yes?"

The thought had come to me as I listened to Hinami and Mizusawa's conversation. I wanted to know. *Those words.*

Up till the night of the barbecue, Mizusawa had looked down on the world from a player's perspective, living life in a way that ensured he was safe from pain. But that night, he broke out of the safe zone and descended to the world of the characters, being true to what he wanted and stepping forward based on his real feelings despite the risk of getting hurt.

It made me wonder—what about me?

The course of action I was planning to take with Kikuchi-san, under instruction from Hinami, wasn't my choice as the character living in this world. No—these were calculated actions chosen by a player who stayed a step removed from the world, a player trying to advance toward an artificial goal called an "assignment." Weren't they?

And that's why I had a suspicion.

"The other day you said I was hard to talk to sometimes, but what about today…?"

Maybe today she felt different.

"Yes. Um, t-today…?"

And if she did, I might have been making a small mistake all along.

"Yes, just today."

That's what I wanted to know.

"Well, now that you mention it…"

A smile spread slowly over Kikuchi-san's face.

"Today, you've been easy to talk to the whole time."

The fireworks had finally reached their climax.

The sky burst with light. The explosion spread outward slowly, gently caressing the darkness and leaving behind glowing trails.

Again and again, until the series of booms and flashes gradually covered the whole night sky with hovering light.

The sky became steadily brighter with each overlapping burst, until everything around us was brightly illuminated. The blinking orange lights that danced around the edge of the whiteness decorated the night sky like strings of Christmas lights.

I couldn't take my eyes off the magical scene.

They say people become more proactive in summer, and it's probably inevitable when things like this are going on. Once you see this brilliant display, you're bound to start feeling a little romantic. I mean, I'd never been in love myself. I'd always turned my eyes away from reality—and even I couldn't help getting the bug.

The trails of light slowly spread from the sky down to the water like a weeping willow tree before melting away. As I watched that last bit of magic, I thought of the assignment Hinami had given me.

[*At the end of the fireworks, tell Kikuchi-san how you feel about her.*]

Another time, she'd told me I'd learned how to take action. I still had trouble acting on my own initiative, but I was able to implement the assignments she gave me.

She was right. I had started conversations with girls, asked Mimimi for her LINE ID, and invited Kikuchi-san to a movie and the fireworks. Before I met Hinami, I couldn't even do that, and now I could. I'd grown.

Maybe it was because the magical light was helping me or maybe it was because the mood was so romantic, but I felt able to say what I had to to complete my current assignment, which was probably the hardest one I'd received so far. I was sure of it.

The last traces of the spell melted into the water, and the sky faded to black again, leaving only the white smoke lit up by the distant skyscrapers. Filled with confidence, I prepared to speak in the lonely, quiet afterglow.

"Kikuchi-san—"

And that confidence was the reason I chose my next words myself.

"—let's go."

* * *

Kikuchi-san and I walked side by side down the crowded street to the station. The wide alley was packed with stalls on either side. Here and there, paper lanterns glowed red. A middle-aged man smiled at the customers as he popped small, round grilled cakes from their molds. A little boy bit into a huge *okonomiyaki* pancake, the sauce smearing the corners of his mouth. A young couple walked along silently, their hands firmly joined. A young woman in a suit, maybe on her way home from work, marched upstream through the crowd with a grumpy look on her face. I walked along simply absorbing each of these scenes, watching Kikuchi-san's expression and movements, experiencing the emotions that arose in response, processing the words and images going through my mind—and I realized something.

At that moment, I was clearly and willfully disobeying Hinami's assignment.

After all, I hadn't felt unable to tell Kikuchi-san my feelings. I simply decided not to.

* * *

After Kikuchi-san and I parted ways, I took the train to Kitayono Station, the nearest one to my house. When I got off the train, I sent a LINE message to Hinami.

[*I finished up a bunch of stuff.*
Can I call you?]

Judging by her response, Hinami must have sensed something unusual in my brief message.

[*If something major happened, should we meet in person?*
I can get to Kitayono fast.]

Apparently, she'd gone to see the fireworks, too, and she was on the Saikyo Line between Toda Koen Station and Omiya Station. If she got off on the way to Omiya, we'd be able to meet right away. I told her that sounded good, and since I was still inside the ticket barrier, I took one of the seats on the platform to wait for her.

Several trains stopped at the platform and departed. When the third or fourth one arrived, I sat in my chair watching the passengers flow out the doors, until eventually I saw a figure peel away from the crowd headed for the stairs and walk in my direction.

It was Hinami.

"...Hey."

"So what happened?"

She looked more serious than usual, but getting right to the point was her typical MO. I stood up, scratched my head, and looked over at the vending machine.

"Wait a second; I'm thirsty. Do you want something?"

"...Not particularly."

"...Okay."

I walked over to the vending machine and bought a can of cold cocoa. Then I sat back down next to Hinami and pulled open the tab.

"So? How did she respond?" she asked in a testing tone.

"Well...," I said, looking straight ahead. "I didn't tell her."

Hinami gave an exasperated sigh. "I know this assignment was one of the harder ones—"

"But not because I couldn't," I interrupted.

"...What?"

She turned quietly to me and stared at my face. I chugged down some cocoa and then looked her in the eye.

"I just decided not to."

I held her gaze, and she held mine.

She was quiet, as if behind her black eyes she was tracing my words back to the intentions motivating them and the logic explaining them and weighing everything. Maybe she was waiting for me to make an excuse, or maybe she wasn't sure what to say in response. In either case, she waited a long, long time, her eyes fixed on mine, but when I said nothing, she finally asked me a question.

"Why?"

She said that single word in an emotionless monotone, expressionless as a mannequin. To me, it sounded as sharp as a knife cutting through the string that tied Hinami and me together. I chose my words carefully but honestly.

"...I went on the date today without memorizing any topics. And I didn't bring up anything I'd memorized before. I only said what came to mind."

"...I see. And?" she asked icily.

"Well, naturally, our conversation wasn't very smooth, and there were long silences, and...it didn't go very well."

"...Obviously." Her face was a total mask.

"But...I asked Kikuchi-san about it at the end. Remember, I told you she'd said after the movie that sometimes I was hard to talk to? Today, I asked her if she felt I was hard to talk to this time. What do you think she said?"

Hinami didn't reply. She just kept looking me in the eye and listening.

"She said, 'Today, you've been easy to talk to the whole time.'"

I waited for her to say something, but when I realized she wasn't going to, I kept going.

"When she first told me I was hard to talk to, I thought she meant my skills weren't developed enough, but that wasn't it at all."

Hinami raised her eyebrows in surprise. I continued.

"The fact was, I was hard to talk to *because* of those skills."

I had been thinking about those words for the past few days now: *"Sometimes you're suddenly very easy to talk to...and sometimes...you're suddenly very hard to talk to."*

I'd assumed that the former was when I smoothly introduced a conversation point from my stock and the latter was when I stumbled and spoke honestly. I mean, I think that was the normal conclusion anyone would reach. That's why I thought I had to work especially hard on memorizing more topics, improving the quality of each one, and stealing techniques for keeping a conversation going. But I'd been completely wrong.

The truth was, I was hard to talk to when I was smooth and easy to talk to when I was more awkward and honest.

I thought back to the conversation between Mizusawa and Hinami.

"...What I think happened was...she saw through the mask I'd created."

I was trying to tell Hinami something very important. So why were her eyes so cold?

"Is that so?" she asked. Her tone was flat and unimpressed. It felt like a rejection of my sincerity.

"...Hinami?"

"There's a countermeasure for that, isn't there? When you're with Kikuchi-san, expressing your true feelings is a more effective attack strategy than memorization—"

"Listen." I interrupted her. "Would you stop doing that?" I was doing everything I could to tell her what I really thought, what I really felt.

"...Doing what exactly?"

She was staring deep into my eyes like she was testing me or trying to see into my mind. I didn't turn away as I answered her.

"Do you really think it's a good idea to start out with countermeasures and attack strategies like you did just now? Don't you think we need to start with questions like, *What do I really want?* or *Do I really like Kikuchi-san?*" She'd left me a tiny opening, and I went for it.

She remained quiet and expressionless for a few moments, then eventually said with disdain, "Did Mizusawa figure you out or something?"

Her cutting tone shocked me. I had carefully poured the truth of my feelings into those words and delivered them with determination—and I had failed to reach her.

"...He did, but..."

True enough, Mizusawa was the catalyst for these thoughts. But that wasn't what I was trying to say.

"...I see," she muttered with the same cold expression. That was all.

"You seem like you want to say something."

She turned her cold gaze away from me. "Not particularly. This is a classic habit of the weak. They're easily misled by the idea of chasing what they really want, when the idea of 'what you really want' doesn't even exist. All it does is hinder forward progress. I'm not surprised to hear it from you." There was no emotion in the delivery of her orderly argument.

"...What's that supposed to mean?"

She gave a tired sigh. "When a person talks about what they really want, simply referring to what happens to be best for them at that particular moment, it's an illusion. Therefore, it's meaningless to let those temporary misconceptions constrain you and distract your focus from truly productive actions."

She gave me another testing look. I thought about it for a moment, and I had to admit her explanation made sense. Everything she said was always correct in some way and scarily stripped of emotion. But was she really, truly *right*?

Was what a person really wanted always a temporary misconception? Was it really unproductive and meaningless to prioritize what you wanted in life over efficiency?

No matter how much I thought about it, I couldn't come up with a logical, rational counterargument for Hinami's point. But based on my intuition, my sense of the issue, and my instincts as nanashi the gamer, I felt like what I really wanted was the most important thing.

"I don't think it's meaningless."

"...What are you talking about?"

I knew insisting I was right wouldn't be able to reach Hinami. Of course not—my point wasn't logical. If we were talking about doing something meaningless—well, this was a case in point.

"...I still want to put what I want first."

Nevertheless, I insisted on it like an idiot.

Yes, what people say they really want can change very easily. You may think you truly want something at one point in time and act accordingly, and then as time passes, the meaning can easily change so you end up contradicting yourself. That's not at all unusual. You could even say it's the norm.

In which case, Hinami's point about what I really wanted being a temporary misconception was actually more logical than my own position. The "correct" thing to do was to avoid letting those thoughts confuse me and instead focus single-mindedly on taking the actions that led to productive, efficient personal growth.

It was an exasperatingly sound argument.

Which meant that nothing else I said would have any effect on her.

Nevertheless, I decided to go with nanashi's instincts.

After all, I'd always changed the rules of the game by using my instincts.

"I think...I need to prioritize what I want."

"I see. And what do you want?"

Her eyes cold, Hinami gave the rational reply to advance the conversation. It made me incredibly sad.

She wasn't asking because she wanted to see the truth in my heart. She was simply searching for a way to advance the conversation.

"You don't want to tell Kikuchi-san you like her because you're not sure about your feelings, right? Well then, would you rather find some other person who meets your standards and set the goal as a confession to them? Who would that be?"

As usual, she was firing logical questions at me. It was like she was still searching for a way for me to avoid my emotional, irrational defects and still achieve the goal. Her proposition was perfectly rational, but it wasn't what I wanted to hear.

"That's...not the issue." I sensed the immense gulf between our values, but I looked her in the eye again.

"Then what is the problem?"

"It's..."

I understood how tremendously important my answer was. I also sensed that Hinami and I might never be able to understand each other on this point. But my only option was to tell her.

"I think it's weird to think of this in terms of assignments and goals... Making friends or telling someone you like them...or any kind of human connection, really."

A train announcement echoed faintly over the nearly deserted platform. Hinami didn't flinch. She just turned her impassive eyes away from me and said, "I see."

"What does that mean?" I asked her.

But she just kept staring wordlessly ahead. Silence fell over us for a moment. Finally, an announcement for an Omiya-bound train played over the loudspeakers, and Hinami quietly answered me.

"Working toward goals was the approach that both of us always took. But if you're going to abandon your goals in life, then you're abandoning your personal improvement."

I felt like she was drawing a line in the sand.

"It's not that. It's...," I tried to argue back, but I couldn't think of anything to say.

"...It's what?"

The way she stared at me as she spoke was somehow unlike her. She seemed to be silently urging me to find the right words to answer her with. But I couldn't find them, and a long silence stretched on.

"...You're different, too, aren't you?"

"Huh?"

For a brief second, she bit her lip as if she was trying to control the sadness surfacing in her eyes. But the next instant, the emotion disappeared like it had never existed, like she had resolved to go another way. She pulled the fireworks pin out of her bag and set it on my knee.

"I'm giving this back, so I want you to give me back the bag I gave you. You can return it next time you see me, since you probably have stuff in it right now. You don't need it anymore, do you?"

I didn't.

I understood what those words meant, and that was why I didn't know how to respond. But if I didn't say anything now, everything would come to an end.

"...But I—"

"Once you drop the controller, you're done for. That's obvious, isn't it?"

Hinami interrupted me and stood up. She was refusing to look at me. Everything she ever said was always correct, so what she was saying now probably was, too. I knew that, but I still felt like I had to disagree, which was why I had told her my thoughts. I'd believed that if I really engaged with her, we would be able to bridge that critical difference, that gap between us—that we had to bridge it. I wanted to find something to bring us together and keep on moving forward. But I didn't have the words, the right answer, to counter Hinami with different but equally sound logic.

And so I simply sat there silently, looking down, watching helplessly as the gap became unbridgeable. Something occurred to me at that moment.

This was happening because I was a bottom-tier character. If only I could communicate my thoughts better, things wouldn't have come to this. If only I could put reason to my ideas, I would have been able to convince her.

For the first time, I felt truly disgusted with myself for my stats.

If I weren't so useless, I wouldn't have had this kind of disagreement and so easily lost the relationships I thought I had established.

Why was I in the bottom tier?
Why was I so *weak*?

It was so incredibly pitiful and frustrating to be such a garbage character in this game. But I knew it was entirely my own fault, because for all these years I hadn't really engaged with life.

I couldn't even bring myself to watch Hinami as she turned away from me and walked onto the train. All I could do was sit there silently, looking down and clenching my fists.

"Well, see you at school."

It was still early August. Summer vacation had barely started. Hinami's good-bye coiled around me with a far greater weight and complexity than the words themselves warranted.

5

Sometimes the characters closest to you end up holding the keys to the toughest dungeons

I was playing *Atafami* like my life depended on it.

I pulled the curtains tight in the middle of the day and cranked up the air conditioner in my dark room, only leaving to eat, take baths, and use the toilet. I didn't even know if one week or two had passed since the night of the fireworks, when Hinami and I talked on the platform. I was so focused on *Atafami* that I lost all sense of time. I'd been too busy to play much lately, but even my pre-Hinami self hadn't played this much in a long time.

"Bang!"

Hinami hadn't contacted me since that night. She hadn't given me any new assignments or checked to see whether I was keeping up with my daily training routine. I guess she didn't feel like it anymore. Which meant I didn't have anything to do aside from *Atafami*.

"Gotcha!"

I played people from all over Japan and gradually increased my rating. That kept me from thinking about anything else.

I felt like I existed in the *Atafami* world instead of the real one.

"Bam!"

But that wasn't anything special. I'd always spent my summer vacations like this. Shut up in a dim room, staring at the glow of my little old CRT TV, playing game after game like my life depended on it.

Before I knew it, my back was hunched, and my mouth was slack and gaping.

"Boom!"

I threw myself into the characters on the TV screen until I was fully absorbed. And it was a blast. I know I'm just a player sitting in front of the screen, but when it came to *Atafami*, I was totally engrossed in trying to get as close as possible to my character.

"Ping!"

Time rushed by even though it felt like it was standing still, and I welcomed it. I wanted to lighten the heavy, complicated chains those words had created around me even a little, so I shut my eyes and curled into a ball and floated in something warm and viscous. But the chains were too heavy, pulling me slowly but surely toward the bottom.

I let that comfortable, sickening sensation seduce me.

I'm not sure how many hours passed. Once again, the sun set without my noticing and the light seeping in between the curtains disappeared. Suddenly, the door opened.

"Sorry, I knocked, but...you're still playing...?"

I turned around. My sister was poking her head in from the living room with her nose wrinkled, like I was something dirty.

"...Huh, what? ...Dinner?"

"Yeah."

"... 'kay."

"Hurry up," she said, walking back into the living room. After a minute, she turned back to look at me. "...Can I ask you something?" She sounded grumpy.

"What...?"

She glared at me. "Why are you turning into a freak again?"

"...Huh?"

"I'm asking you a question!" She stomped her foot and scowled. "Why do you look like you did a couple of months ago?!"

I felt like I knew what she meant, but I just nodded vaguely. "What can I say?"

"Grrr! And you were so much better, too!" She slammed the door violently.

"Whoa...," I whimpered. I wasn't sure what to do, but I stood up and opened the door to go into the living room. My sister was still standing like a statue in front of the door.

"Okay, so when you brought those cool kids over and called them your friends, I wondered if you were really my brother."

"Huh?"

She was glaring at me fiercely.

"But it's *really* not like you to look so bored staring at your games."

With that, she strode over to her chair at the table and glared at the TV.

Her words had cleared away a little of the fog in my mind. Huh. So I had looked bored when I was playing *Atafami* just now? Not good. Still, I felt so wishy-washy. I didn't know where to look or where to stand.

I looked around. Dad wasn't home. Mom was in the kitchen cleaning up. I sat down unsteadily at the table. My sister glared at me and started talking again—apparently, she'd forgotten something.

"...And also!"

She pressed the phone I'd left lying in the living room for the past few days to my chest.

"Huh...?"

"It's not like you to ghost a girl on LINE! You're getting a little full of yourself, I'd say."

"Huh?"

That was a surprise to hear. I'd been getting messages from a girl? Someone must have contacted me in the past few days. But who? ...Probably not Hinami. I glanced at the screen of my phone and saw a two-day-old LINE notification.

[Kind Dogs Stand Alone *comes out on the twenty-first.*
I'm planning to buy a copy from a bookstore in Omiya.
Would you like to come?]

As soon as I realized it was an invitation from Kikuchi-san, a wave of regret and guilt washed over me.

She'd sent it two days ago.

What the hell was I doing?

Assuming Kikuchi-san was like me, sending a message like this to a classmate of the opposite gender couldn't have been easy. Not even if the recipient was the lowest-tier character in our school.

And I'd let it sit for two days.

First, I'd actively pursued her for my "assignments" and "goals," and then I'd turned around and shut her out when she took the initiative in asking me to do something.

What a jerk.

I'd told Hinami it was weird to interact with people for the sake of assignments and goals, that I had to be truer to what I really wanted. I'd rebelled against her for that idea, and then I went off and did this. I was full of it.

However you looked at it, I was incredibly self-centered.

Once again, I was disgusted by my own bottom-tier behavior. Had I defied Hinami just so I could act this way?

I looked at the LINE message again.

No, this definitely wasn't why I'd done it. In which case, I should at least make an honest attempt to act according to my own ideas. The realization spread across my foggy brain, and I started composing a message to Kikuchi-san.

So what *did* I want? At the very least, I needed to base my actions on that.

As I began to write, my mood was still dark, but I was fighting my way into the light.

[*I'm sorry! I haven't checked my phone in a while! Do you still want to go on the twenty-first?*]

It took all my energy, but I managed to type that up. The one thing I didn't want to do was run away from seeing her again. An assignment or goal may have started everything, but Kikuchi-san still decided to get involved with me, and it was wrong not to take her seriously. I didn't want to distance myself from people I'd connected with anymore. That was the weak-willed, passive approach; in this case, my feeling that I needed to keep things going won out. Plus, I decided this was what I really wanted in the current situation.

I sent the message and turned off my screen. When I took a deep breath and glanced to the side, I saw that my sister was staring at me.

"...What?"

She made a silly face and shrugged her shoulders.

"Sometimes...life is tough. Just do your best, all right?" she said theatrically. I think she was trying to irritate me.

"...Right... Thanks."

Just this once, though, I wanted to express my appreciation.

* * *

On the twenty-first, I went to Omiya Station.

What did I want to say to Kikuchi-san? I had no idea.

I thought about what I'd said to Hinami, and I wasn't sure what would happen with her. I'd defied her to get across my feelings about doing what I wanted, but was I right? Or was she right, and I was pursuing an illusion and a temporary misconception?

Those were the questions knocking around in my mind as I walked through Omiya Station inside the ticket gate. I didn't really feel like going anywhere, but I'd decided to come anyway.

I got to the place where we'd agreed to meet and looked around. My eyes were immediately drawn to a certain spot, and there was Kikuchi-san, elegant yet striking among the crowd. I walked up to her.

"...Hi."

"...Hello."

Her greeting, which came after an odd pause, was somehow comforting. I'd felt like my heart had been trapped in a large cold box until now, and warmth came flooding in all at once.

"Um, sh-shall we?"

I didn't use any of my conversation skills, and I knew my words and gestures must have seemed halting, but I was frantic to say something. There was a lot I didn't know, and my thoughts were very scattered. But my first task was to deal with the business at hand.

"...Yes, let's go!"

We were headed to a bookstore in the SOGO shopping complex

outside the west exit of Omiya Station. Just like at the fireworks, I had decided not to use any memorized topics to smooth out the conversation or try to stock up EXP. For the current me, that was the most sincere thing I could manage. It was also just what I wanted to do.

I wasn't wearing any of the clothes Hinami had chosen for me, either. I felt like they were their own kind of mask.

"I'm really looking forward to this…!" Kikuchi-san's eyes glittered as she talked about Andi's newly published book. She apparently couldn't care less about my dorky outfit.

"Yeah. I wonder what the story of this one's gonna be like…"

"It's impossible to tell from the title, isn't it?"

"True…but the title feels a little different from the others, don't you think?"

"Yes, I thought the same thing…"

"…Yeah."

"…Uh-huh."

The conversation fizzled out. We walked quietly for a while. The plain old me was exposed, without any made-up fronts or airs. If I wasn't mistaken, though, that didn't seem to make Kikuchi-san feel awkward. We cut through the station, and as we walked outside through the west exit, she pulled on a black cardigan.

"Oh right… You always put that on when you're outside, right?"

"Yes…" She nodded, blushing a little.

"You're not hot?"

"I'm a little warm, but…when I get a sunburn, it just feels even hotter. Plus it stings."

"Ah-ha-ha…yeah, that sounds really uncomfortable."

The exchange ended. That was how it went—there were long pauses now and then, and I was clumsy, but the conversation never truly died. I talked about myself, and if I was curious about something, I asked Kikuchi-san.

I didn't feel uncomfortable. I was interacting with her based strictly on my true feelings. When I thought about it, that was what I'd always done until recently.

"...So recently, I've just been playing *Atafami* at home all the time."

Kikuchi-san giggled. "All I've been doing is reading..."

"Ah-ha-ha. You're an indoor type, huh?"

"Seems like you are, too!" Kikuchi-san sounded a little excited. Then she giggled again, and I couldn't help laughing, too.

Our insignificant conversation jolted along. It didn't matter if an exchange faded or if my clothes were dorky or if I played *Atafami* at home all the time. Kikuchi-san accepted it all and responded honestly.

And she thought the real me was easy to talk to. That alone was enough to thaw some of the chill in my heart.

After walking for a while, we came to the SOGO building.

"Aah, it's so cool," I said as we got into the elevator and rode up toward the bookstore.

"I love how bookstores smell," Kikuchi-san whispered, breaking into a gentle smile as we stepped out of the elevator. To me, her steps looked just a little lighter than usual, like a forest fairy flitting happily from one branch to the next.

"Really?"

It had never occurred to me to love the smell of a bookstore, but it seemed extremely fitting for Kikuchi-san. Maybe the reason she looked so elegant no matter what she wore and had that outstanding magical power was that she routinely recharged her MP by surrounding herself with books.

I walked behind her as she excitedly ogled the bookshelves and signs. It struck me as unusual for her to walk ahead so independently. She really did love books.

"Oh, look!" she exclaimed, slipping into a row of shelves.

"What?"

She was leaning in close to a lineup of teen romances.

"This one was amazing!" she said, entranced as she gazed at the cover of the book she'd pulled off the shelf. Not exactly what I was expecting.

"Huh... You read this stuff?"

"Uh...um, yes... I do..." She blushed and stiffened.

"Oh, s-sorry…it's just not quite what I would have guessed."

"Actually, I—I…," she said, looking down. "I'd like to write books like this one day." She was clamming up, her cheeks red and her eyes glistening.

"…Um, r-really?"

"Um…y-yes."

Flustered, she returned the book to the shelf and started walking a step behind me. But soon it happened again.

"Oh!" She pattered down another aisle and gazed at the bookshelf. "I've read this so many times…"

"You have?"

And again.

"Oh! …This was such a fun read."

Over and over. I found it endearing, but I also wanted to take her comments about the books seriously. Up till now, I'd always seen her as a fairy or an angel, but now that we'd hung out a few times, I realized she was the most honest, straightforward girl I knew. Her entire life centered around what she really wanted.

After a few minutes, we came to the shelf that held *Kind Dogs Stand Alone.*

"Here it is!"

"Wow…"

She leaped in front of me with glittering eyes, pulled the book off the shelf, and began to examine the front cover, spine, and back with such intense emotion—something like surprise. Then she devoted the same attention to the inner flaps.

"…I feel like I'm dreaming," she said softly, holding the book in front of her chest with both hands and gazing at it.

Her emotional tone, expression, and gestures struck straight at my heart. After a few moments, I gradually realized why it was getting to me so much—Kikuchi-san's devotion to what she wanted was pierced through with a quiet strength that was not only entirely natural but essential to her way of life. Without exaggeration, she was living every second of her life as a character.

"...Yeah."

I nodded. We each took a copy of the book and walked over to the register to pay.

* * *

"I come here a lot after work," Kikuchi-san said.

After buying our books, we'd walked over to a café near the east exit of the station. Maybe because the atmosphere was calming for her or maybe because she felt satisfied after buying the book, her expression was more serene and relaxed than usual as she sat primly in her chair.

"Everything on the menu sounds so good."

"It is!" Kikuchi-san said happily and a little more loudly than usual. "...And it's all so pretty."

All the pictures on the menu were gorgeous. The red tomatoes, yellow peppers, green parsley and asparagus, and everything else was colorful and appetizing. The whole place suited Kikuchi-san perfectly.

We eventually both decided to order rice-stuffed omelets.

"I can't believe I finally got to buy it!"

"...Yeah."

Kikuchi-san hadn't put the book in her purse since buying it. Instead, she'd carried the plastic bag in her hands as we walked and had now set it on the table next to her. She was treating it so carefully.

The conversation broke off abruptly again. There was no sign of our meal.

"I'm gonna run to the bathroom," I said, standing up. I'd had a hard time saying even that when I was surrounded by normies, but with Kikuchi-san, it felt natural and easy. That made a big impression on me. Just another reminder of how I could be myself around her.

I got to the bathroom; took care of business, casual and content; and went over to the sink to wash my hands. That's when it happened.

I saw myself in the mirror.

I'd made a point of coming in my natural state today, so I hadn't paid attention to what clothes I wore, and I hadn't put wax in my hair. I hadn't even looked in the mirror before leaving the house. Dressing up had struck me as just another "skill" for lying about who I was. Now the results were staring me in the face.

I looked like a gross gamer nerd.

My posture was slouched, the corners of my mouth were drooping, I looked dirty, my clothes were definitely not stylish, and my eyes were dull.
I was disgusted with myself.

I'd gotten used to seeing my hair spiffed up with wax, so the flat non-style with tufts sticking out here and there just looked dirty and lazy.

Hinami had taught me to pay attention to what I wore, so the wrinkly, baggy clothes that I used to wear without a second thought stood out almost shockingly.

It had become a habit to stand up straight and lift the corners of my mouth, so my expression and posture struck me as weak, childish, and hollow. To take it to an extreme, they made me sick.

I didn't recognize myself.

What did I want to become? Hinami's words as we parted ways on the platform echoed in my mind.

"If you're going to abandon your goals in life, then you're abandoning your personal improvement."

I'd believed that improving myself by carrying out goals established from a player's perspective, like the ones Hinami gave me, wasn't what I really wanted to do. I'd thought I had to improve myself by doing what I really wanted. I'd concluded that the improvements I'd gained by reaching those player-perspective goals—things like dressing nicely, consciously making facial expressions, and styling my hair—were meaningless.

I'd come to see those kinds of improvements as nothing more than a mask, and that was why I'd come dressed in my nerdy old clothes and bedhead today. I was even trying *not* to stand up straight or adjust my expression.

I thought that was what it meant to be true to myself. But just now, when I saw myself in the mirror, it wasn't my player self judging from a distance the impression I gave.

It was the character—Fumiya Tomozaki, living in the real world—who didn't like how I looked.

I remembered the day I went to buy Nakamura a present with Mizusawa, Izumi, and Hinami. I'd glanced in the mirror as we were going down the escalator and seen myself. I looked like a normie. I'd felt uplifted, happy, and genuinely motivated. And not only then. The time Mizusawa, Mimimi, and Hinami came to my house, the smooth conversation we'd had had given me a powerful sense of accomplishment.

In other words, when I improved myself by working toward goals I'd set from a player's perspective, the character living in the real world had felt genuine happiness. That real-world character had been happy to improve.

But somehow, I'd convinced myself that anything I gained by reaching player-perspective goals was meaningless.

What the hell did I want?

I felt that life was meaningless if I didn't stay true to what I really wanted on the one hand, but how could I reconcile that belief with the meaning I'd found from accomplishing those player-perspective goals?

Was it okay not to base my actions on what my heart was telling me?

* * *

I didn't know. Part of me instinctively wanted to prioritize my own desires, while another part felt it was meaningful to take a step back and work to become a better person.

I left the bathroom still mulling over that strange contradiction, with no answers in sight.

* * *

"Oh, the food came?"

"Yes!"

Kikuchi-san's omelet was still untouched. She must have been waiting for me to come back. I wouldn't have cared if she'd started without me, but I was still oddly happy she'd waited. I sat down and thought about what to do as we both dug in.

Finally, I looked up at her. Was I being overly dependent? I was about to ask her for advice. She was entirely focused on what she wanted, and she'd seen through my little mask immediately—but still accepted me as I was. And her willingness to accept me was why I wanted to talk to her.

"…Um…"

"…Yes?" Kikuchi-san responded slowly, like I would have. It was comforting, and I couldn't help taking advantage of it. She was so easy to talk to.

"Um…remember how, after the movie, you said that sometimes I was hard to talk to and sometimes I was easy to talk to?"

"Oh, uh-huh…"

She nodded, looking a little surprised, probably because I was bringing it up again.

"Well, I think there's…a reason for that," I said, hesitating just a little. I was about to reveal my mask to her.

"Lately…someone has been coaching me on how to talk and things like that… I've been using a recorder to check whether my voice is coming out like I think it is, and copying people in class like…like Mizusawa, and other stuff like that."

The only thing I kept secret was Hinami's name.

"Someone…" Kikuchi-san zeroed in on that point as she listened to me seriously.

"And as one part of that training… Well, you can't start a conversation without something to talk about, right? So I made flash cards for each person…with topics on them that I memorized…" I was afraid she wouldn't like me once she knew that, which was why I kind of trailed off at the end, but I still managed to keep talking. "Before we went to the movies together…I made a bunch of those cards about things like 'Hinami's clothes' and 'the details of what happened with Mimimi,' and I memorized them so I could actually use them when we were together."

"…Oh."

As I expected, Kikuchi-san looked somewhat surprised, but she kept listening earnestly, looking me in the eye.

"But at the fireworks and today, I didn't use any memorized topics or make an effort to keep the conversation going. And you said I was easier to talk to these two times."

"…So that's what was going on." She smiled kindly, like she was satisfied with my explanation.

"I figured that when I used those cheap tricks to make conversation, there was something unnatural about it…and that's what made you feel like I was hard to talk to. I thought it was because you'd seen through my mask and realized I was insincere."

I searched for the words as if I were gathering up the emotions that had sunk to the bottom of my heart.

"But…when I used that mask or those skills with Mizusawa and Hinami and Mimimi, and it made the conversation go more smoothly, I felt a sense of accomplishment. And that wasn't fake. It was a genuine sense of accomplishment."

"I see…" Kikuchi-san nodded several times as she listened.

"So I really don't know if I should keep working on those skills or if I should just be myself. I'm not sure which one is closer to what I really want."

Kikuchi-san looked down, like she wasn't sure what to say. Suddenly, I snapped back to reality.

"Oh…sorry for talking about all this weird stuff all of a sudden. I'm sure this makes no sense."

Once again, I was regretting my actions. Why was I acting so weak and unfair? Since Kikuchi-san accepted everything about me, maybe I just wanted her to accept the weak parts of myself that I hated. I wondered what I else should say to her. She was still looking down.

But when she lifted her face up a second later, her expression was strong and kind.

"…I…" She looked me in the eye. "The reason I think you're easy to talk to…is that I can picture what you're saying."

"…You can picture it? …How?"

That came out of left field.

Kikuchi-san nodded deeply. "A lot of the time, I feel like you directly say whatever pops into your head…and when you do that, an image pops into my head, too, although I'm not sure if it's the same as the one you have. It's just like…I'm reading a novel."

"How so?" I glanced at the book on the table in its plastic bag.

"Well…I don't mean that your sentences sound like prose… It's more like the things you've seen come across to me unprocessed. I feel like you're directly, honestly relaying whatever mood or emotion or texture you noticed."

As she talked, Kikuchi-san slowly moved both of her hands like she was shaping a sculpture in midair.

"I think that's your personality…and that's why you're easy to talk to…"

"Th-thank you…"

"Oh, uh-huh…" Although she was blushing now, Kikuchi-san kept explaining. "But sometimes the picture doesn't come across very clearly… and I was thinking just now, those are probably the times you were using the topics you memorized from the cards…"

"Oh yeah…"

Her point was slowly coming into focus.

"And I think that's what makes you hard to talk to."

That was why she had looked satisfied a few minutes earlier. But that meant…

"So you think making an effort to develop those skills is a bad idea…?"

"Not necessarily." Kikuchi-san looked at me. Her earnest, shining eyes pulled me in.

"...Really?"

She smiled like a goddess overflowing with gentle affection. "I do think you've changed a lot lately... Being hard to talk to sometimes is part of it...but it's more than that..."

"More than that?" Other changes? What had changed aside from my skills?

"Ever since the first time we talked, I've found it interesting that I'd get these images when you're talking."

"...Uh-huh."

I nodded, as if her words were drawing me toward her.

"...But the images were all in black and white."

"...Oh."

Once again, she completely surprised me.

"When I talk to you, your colorless world feels a little lonely, but in a certain way...it's similar to the world that I see."

"What...do you see?"

Kikuchi-san stared at her palms, then smiled a little sadly. "Sometimes...the world I see when I'm reading books looks more beautiful than the real world in front of me. Every time I read a book that makes me feel that way, I'm jealous of the author. After all, the world must look so colorful to them..."

She gently patted the book inside the plastic bag.

"Especially Andi's books," she said with a smile. "And...the world that appears when I talk to you is black and white...like mine... So when I heard that you like to play *Atafami*...I wondered if the world of that game is filled with color for you, just like the world in books is for me."

"...Yeah." I think she was right. The reality I'd written off as a shitty game did feel like it was all in gray, and diving into the world of *Atafami* was full of color by comparison. "I think that's true."

"But...you know what?" she said as if she were about to gently correct me, gazing quietly at me. "As we talked more...and you talked about your life, the images that I saw..."

She sounded as if she were reading a classic children's story to me.

"...I could see the color coming in."

I felt as if she were picking up a very important part of my heart that I had happened to drop at her feet; I think I already understood what she was getting at.

"That really surprised me," she continued. "Ever since I was a little girl, the world I saw was gray. Nothing changed when I got to high school... so I thought it would always be the same. That it would always be gray."

"Yeah..." I knew that feeling.

"But over a very short period of time, you—"

She must be talking about the crazy changes I'd gone through in the past few months.

"—you managed to change the color of the world you see."

Yes. Exactly.

I'd always seen the world as the worst kind of a game, a stupid conspiracy created by the normies—but lately, I'd been making an effort to improve my ability in it, one step at a time. I'd gradually been changing my environment, and as I did, my relationships with other people transformed, too. My prejudices faded, and my experience of the world had become something new. The effort I invested in the real world allowed me to do more things and transformed my surroundings.

But more than that, the color of the world I saw was completely different now.

It hit me with crystal clarity that this change was something truly precious.

I listened, absorbed and silent, to Kikuchi-san's words.

"That's why I think it's really wonderful that you're making an effort to change yourself," she said, and her smile seemed to embrace the whole world.

"Oh...you do?" It was like I'd just taken a full-body blow, and all I could do was nod. I felt like the answer I'd been searching for was there in Kikuchi-san's words.

"Maybe...you're right," I said haltingly.

"Also, this is just a maybe, but...," she said, looking down pensively, as if an idea had just occurred to her.

"...Yeah?"

She pulled the Michael Andi book out of its plastic bag. "If there's a wonderful, magical person in your life," she said, hugging the book softly to her chest. "Someone who's painted your gray world in color..."

She looked straight at me and smiled a warm, direct, very human smile.

"Then I think you should treasure that relationship."

Once again, she'd taught me something important. For a long moment, I couldn't stop staring at her. Then finally...

"...Yeah. Thank you, Kikuchi-san."

I wanted to communicate the deep, heartfelt gratitude I was experiencing to her, so I used my "serious tone skill" to thank her.

She shook her head kindly.

"Consider it a small thanks for showing me that it's not too late for me to change how I see the world." She smiled.

Maybe I was seeing things, but I swear the twinkle in her eyes was a color that was just a little different from usual.

6

Equipment for girls has special effects

After I said good-bye to Kikuchi-san at Omiya Station, I went home, took out my phone, and opened another LINE conversation for the first time in two weeks.

I had to tell that certain person who always saw the world from a player's perspective—I had to share with her the valuable lesson Kikuchi-san had taught me. After all, I really didn't want things to end like this.

[*I'm sorry*
I want to talk one more time
Can we meet up somewhere soon?]

I sent the message and waited for Hinami's reply. About fifteen minutes passed.

[*Talk about what?*]

I could sense the rejection in her short, emotionless message. But I'd already decided to move forward. And I'd made up my mind that I wouldn't hesitate to use my "skills."

[*I've been thinking a lot*
I want to talk again]

The notification saying she'd read my message popped up right away.

[*There's nothing I want to talk about.*]

Her reply was cold, but I charged ahead; I knew what I wanted to do here.

[*You told me to give you back your bag, didn't you?*]

Maybe because she wasn't expecting me to say that, there was a pause between the "read" notification and her reply.

[*I did say that.*]

[*It'll be a hassle to bring it to school*
One more thing to carry]

[*Are you kidding me?*]

I could imagine her exasperated expression.

[*Let me return it during summer vacation*]

I sent another message.

[*Otherwise I might not be able to give it back*]

She read it right away. Of course, none of what I'd written was actually true. But Hinami had told me once that in order to achieve a goal and get my opinion across, I might have to put on a false front. If I didn't, I'd never achieve anything. Well then, I'd do it now. I'd fight in her ring.

Given her tendency to value sound logic, she'd probably have a hard time turning me down. A minute or two passed.

[*In that case, you can keep it.*]

What? That was her strategy? She'd caught me off guard. As I started to rack my brain for a new angle of attack, another message arrived from Hinami.

[*But if you want to meet that badly*
Tomorrow at six. Omiya.]

I did a little fist pump. I couldn't deny feeling she'd given some ground, but the important thing was reaching my goal. It would be worse to give her any less than my best.

[*Okay.*]

I waited until the "read" notification arrived, then turned off my phone. I started to put my thoughts in order for our meeting tomorrow, reflecting once again on what I really wanted.

* * *

The next day, I took Hinami's bag and headed for Omiya. My back was straight, my mouth firm, my hair styled, and I was wearing an outfit she had selected.

It wasn't a mask. It was the armor I needed for our encounter.

We were meeting at six. I got to the Bean Tree sculpture at 5:55 and waited for her with an uncomfortable combination of restless anxiety and determination.

She arrived exactly at six. She stopped directly in front of me and just looked me in the eyes. She wasn't glaring at me or assessing me this time. I decided to speak first to prevent that look from undercutting my momentum.

"This isn't the best place to talk. Wanna go somewhere else?"

Without waiting for her answer, I started walking toward the east exit. Hinami silently followed a step behind with her perfect, disciplined stride. After we'd walked for a few minutes, I realized something.

"...Oh."

I stopped in front of a convenience store. It was a completely ordinary convenience store near the station with nothing whatsoever to distinguish it. But for me, it was the place where everything began. This was the convenience store where NO NAME and I had arranged to meet in person for the first time.

It was the place where I first talked to the "real" Hinami.

My feet had naturally stopped in front of the store. We could have talked anywhere, but for no real reason, I decided this would be a good place. I turned back to Hinami and took a deep breath.

"...What I wanted to talk to you about was—" I was ready to dive in.

"Did you think of a new excuse or something?" Hinami interrupted with a blank expression, as I would have predicted.

But I didn't want that to beat me, so I hurried to keep talking.

"It's not an excuse. I realized something."

"Realized what?"

I thought back to the things I'd learned from Kikuchi-san, and to be fair, the things I'd learned and received from Hinami. Then I told her the answer I'd arrived at.

"I like video games."

"...Well, that's breaking news." She looked at me suspiciously.

"I like *Atafami*, and I like RPGs. And I liked playing the game of the student council election against you so much I'd happily do it again if I could. Even if it was partially my fault Mimimi had to go through what she did."

One by one, I transformed my true feelings into words, almost giving them physical shape.

"...Is that so?" Hinami's expression did not change.

I recalled my gray memories of not so long ago.

"But in *Atafami*, I'm always a player. I'm on the outside, sitting in front of the TV, holding my controller and moving my character on the screen. There's no way I can get any closer."

"Obviously."

I nodded. "But I still poured my soul into it because I wanted to become one with my character. The closer I was, the more exciting the world inside the game was."

I was getting emotional.

"The reason I was drawn to games more than anime or novels or manga...the reason the game world sucks me in more than anything else...is simple."

Games have one unique characteristic that none of those other media share.

"*At least in a game*, I can make my character do whatever I want."

Only in games could I be a top-tier character. My character's experiences became mine, and that was why that world was so fascinating to me. I mean, in a game, I didn't have to experience my own weakness or pitifulness or the crushing, irrational hatred I had toward myself for being me. In that sense, you could say that I lived more as my characters than I did in the real world.

"That's the draw of the game world. I thought the real world was a shitty game. Nothing about it was fun, because I couldn't manipulate the character Fumiya Tomozaki how I wanted to."

I thought back again to the gray life of a few months ago.

"I didn't mean to mumble, but when I listened to a recording of myself, I realized that's what I was doing. I didn't mean to turn down the corners of my mouth, but when you shoved that mirror in my face, I saw that's what I was doing. I didn't mean to have such bad posture, and I didn't stutter because I liked to."

More than anything else, that was what made my life gray. And I never would have figured it out on my own.

"But how could I make my voice sound the way I wanted? How could I make my expression look how I wanted? How could I have the posture I wanted—how could I make my character act the way I imagined? All those techniques for playing the game of life, for making real life into something exciting—"

I tried to speak from the depths of my soul.

"I learned because you took the time to teach me."

Memories flooded my mind. You could call them images from the new landscape that Hinami showed me, full of colors I hadn't known existed a few months earlier.

The happiness on the face of my "student" when she told me she'd gotten better at *Atafami*. The sunny smile Mimimi gave me after I'd struggled in my own clumsy way to help her solve her problems. The primitive yet piercing elation I felt when I realized I'd leveled up. That incredibly fun, silly, lively barbecue. The strange, satisfying, embarrassing sense of solidarity after we'd succeeded in bringing Nakamura and Izumi a little closer together. The warm, happy feeling like snow melting that I got when Kikuchi-san and I had a deep conversation.

All those memories sparkled brilliantly like colored lights decorating the dark night sky, burning their afterimage slowly but surely into my world.

It felt like magic.

"I want to be a character in real life, because thanks to you, I'm starting to like this game, too."

That wasn't a lie. There was no way I could deny the appeal of the work I'd put in and the experiences I'd had since meeting her or the ways my surroundings had changed as a result. Same goes for all the new amazing moments that had made the real world more interesting and the colorful magic she'd sprinkled over my life.

True, things didn't go how I expected them to more often than not, and sometimes I still felt uncomfortable. At times, my own weakness had gotten me hurt, and I thought my heart was going to shatter into a thousand pieces. But I still wanted to be a character in this game. After all, I'm the top gamer in Japan! I never go halfway on games that I like.

"That's what I really want to do."

I waited for Hinami to respond. In the end, what I really wanted was to keep the same stance I'd always had as a gamer.

I wanted to throw myself fully into this game I'd come to like and enjoy it to the fullest. And because I liked it, I wanted my character to be deeper and more real than anyone else's.

I'm pretty sure that was the only answer I could have given Hinami that was different from hers but still correct.

But after a pause, Hinami shook her head.

"This idea you have about what you really want—there's no such thing." She was rejecting everything I'd just said. "You're just letting yourself get idealistic and sentimental."

I understood that this, too, was correct.

"You seem to think that becoming a character is what you really want, but it's not. Your emotions are getting the better of you, and you've mistaken that for your ideal. You're giving it more weight than it deserves."

Her tone was as cool as ever. She wasn't budging.

"If that's what you genuinely want to pursue, then you have to prove it and stick to it. Otherwise, it's meaningless."

Looking back, she could see all the logic she'd used, the actions she'd taken, and the results she'd reaped. Her confidence was based on those accumulated outcomes. That was why she believed so firmly that she was right.

Her confidence was built on results.

Effort led gradually to outcomes, which led to confidence, which became strength. That's what I'd sensed, on a very minor scale, when I "leveled up." And since Hinami had more results to look back on than anyone else, she was a stronger character than anyone else.

But if I took the opposite perspective…

"I thought you'd say that."

If I was able to break down that argument…

"And you're right that I have to prove it or else it's meaningless."

Then that would be the surest counterattack possible against Hinami.

She was momentarily silent in the face of my confident reply.

"Are you trying to say you can prove it?" she finally asked, looking at me sharply.

Maybe I was wrong, but I didn't sense any animosity in her eyes.

"What I really want does exist. I'm sure of it," I declared. I knew that was what she expected me to say.

"…Really now." For the first time, she smiled. "Tell me then, what's your evidence?"

I smiled back at her. "What are you talking about? You really don't get it, do you?"

"…Huh?" she said, clearly very confused.

Now that I had her running, I attacked again.

"I mean, proving what you really want is a function of simple rules, and they intersect in complex ways. They're not that easy to teach."

It was a logical argument—one she'd once made to me when I was first climbing into her ring. For a few seconds, she froze, stunned, until she gave a small, shocked laugh.

"Ha… So what do you plan to do?"

"It's obvious, isn't it?" I replied jokingly. "When you buy a new game and bring it home, how do you get good at it?"

That, too, was one of her own logical arguments. She'd been explaining the most rational, efficient method for improvement. She could see what I was doing, and she sighed.

"...I know, I know—you try playing it."

I nodded. "Right. You're not going to find what you really want by asking for evidence that it exists. You have to struggle to discover how you feel and move forward in earnest—only then."

Hinami furrowed her eyebrows. "You..."

"Listen, Hinami," I said with the confidence of a teacher about to deliver an important lesson. "You're good at managing your life, but that's all you do. You always look at the world from a player's perspective. I don't think you know what real fun is." I was trying to get a rise out of her.

"...What is with you?"

"Just listen," I declared. "I'm going to tell you something. You're a top-tier character, that's true. But when it comes to enjoying the game of life, I'm ahead of you now."

Hinami smiled, unfazed. "What?"

I pointed at her. "Starting today, I'm gonna teach you step-by-step how to really throw yourself into the game. How can you discover what you really want? How can you get more fun out of life? Of course, I'm not as good as you at putting rules into words, so this will probably be a slow process."

Hinami tilted her head somewhat theatrically. "Where do you get off lecturing me like that? You keep talking about these true desires or whatever, and I don't even believe they exist. The closest you get is wishful thinking or a whim. Shouldn't you start there?"

I nodded. "Maybe. But try thinking of it like this."

She rested her cheek in her hand with interest and smiled combatively. "...Like what?"

"For me, those true desires have always fueled my drive to play games."

"...Pfft."

I stuck my pointer finger in the air.

"That's how I got to be the top *Atafami* player in Japan—and you haven't beaten me."

* * *

Just for an instant, shock crossed Hinami's face.

"Don't you think it's strange? You're number one in academics, sports, the school hierarchy, and most other games. But in *Atafami*, you just can't get the top spot. We know the effect, so now we just need the cause, right?"

For every effect there is a cause—that's one of the rules that makes up the game of reality.

That's the unshakable view of games that Hinami and I share.

"Of course, but it has to do with the level of effort—"

"You're wrong."

I cut her off, wagging my finger.

"...Then what?" she said, grabbing my finger before it could offend her further.

"Haven't you guessed yet? The thing that makes me better than you at *Atafami*—"

I pointed at her again.

"—is that I know what I really want, and you don't."

"...Oh reall—"

I cut her off again. "The fact is, you haven't beaten me. And that's the best evidence around that I might be on to something. Of course, I can see that because I'm the top *Atafami* player in Japan, but you might not understand." I grinned to hammer home the point. "If that's frustrating for you, just try beating me at *Atafami* without knowing what you really want."

I beckoned to her with my finger, inviting her counterargument.

"No..." She started to argue back but eventually seemed to give up on continuing.

Of course she did. I mean, her superstrong fighting style was to climb into the ring someone else had made and obliterate them head-on through sheer effort. After all the work she poured into her goal, she never lost to anyone.

But I'm different.

She and I aren't just Fumiya Tomozaki and Aoi Hinami.

On a deeper level than that, we're nanashi and NO NAME.

But this particular arena is built from things you can only know when you master *Atafami*; it's illogical and unfair, but here you're only allowed to complain once you beat me. And here, I and I alone am guaranteed to win.

Of course, I'll admit I made that ring specifically to reach my own goals, and originally it revolved entirely around me. It was inaccessible to anyone else.

Until she came along.

After all, she's always chosen to get into her opponent's ring and crush them head-on. She hates to lose with every cell in her body.

"...I see," she said with a tired sigh.

"What?"

"Given you're trying to prove something that doesn't exist, your empty logic isn't half-bad."

"E-empty...?"

Hinami gave a half-impressed, half-disgusted little laugh.

"You're right; I can't come up with a counterargument. On the other hand, you haven't proven anything."

"Point taken."

I yielded with a nod. Just because I'd argued that she wasn't able to understand my point by putting it into a barely convincing context, that didn't prove anything.

"Ultimately, it's impossible to say who's right, so I'll meet you halfway. I'm not accepting that people have some secret deep thing that they ultimately want, but I'll agree that it's wrong to assume they don't."

At long last, for the very first time, Aoi Hinami bent just a little. I couldn't help smiling.

"Hinami..."

"But," she said severely, pointing at me. "If you're going to argue that hard, then you'd better put the time into proving it. Convince me beyond a shadow of a doubt."

That struck me as an impossibly hard assignment. But if I was going to follow through on what I really wanted and stay involved with this terrifyingly rational perfectionist at the same time, then I had no choice but to obey.

"...Right. Got it."

Once she had my promise, her face softened, and a moment later, that expression turned to exhaustion as she pressed her palm to her forehead.

"...So..."

"...What?"

"Nothing... I was just wondering what you want to do from here on out."

For once, there was no energy in her voice.

"Oh right."

Yeah, that was the question. I'd rejected her checklist of goals, so what did I want our relationship to be like now? I hadn't told her yet, but of course I already had an answer. All I had to do was say it.

"I...want to keep on trying to beat this game. Just like I've done so far."

I genuinely did want to stick with her attack strategy.

"...Really?" Unusually for her, she looked away. A tiny, vaguely awkward smile played at her lips.

"The skills you've been teaching me are necessary to become a real character, and they don't contradict what I really want, so I'd like to continue."

"...But sometimes they do, right?"

I nodded. "Yes, and when that happens, I want to opt out."

"Essentially...you want to use the skills but construct the goals based on what you really want?"

Hinami frowned. Apparently, she was tired of my selfishness.

"More or less. Basically—"

I thought back to what Mizusawa had said to me at Tenya.

"—my playing style is a hybrid of skills and true feelings."

I looked Hinami in the eye and grinned. She sighed again and muttered that if I was that confident, I'd better come up with some proof.

"Well, I'm not superconfident, but—leave it to me, NO NAME."

As I spoke, I channeled my favorite character in my favorite game and raised my right arm in an imitation of his Attack pose. After all, Hinami and I had a way of communicating that was way faster and better than words. She sighed, predictably fed up but also slightly happy, I think.

"Okay then, I'm not expecting much, but I'll leave it to you, nanashi."

She raised her right arm, a little reluctantly. I recognized the familiar sadism in her half smile. Yeah, that was the expression that suited her best.

We both relaxed our fists at the same time. Neither of us was trying to prove we were right or deny our weakness. Instead, we were slowly approaching each other so that eventually our ideals would link up. Finally...

Our palms met softly in midair.

* * *

We'd talked a lot, and my brain was dead, so at my suggestion, we walked over to a diner nearby.

"I think I'll get the salted mackerel set," I said.

"What a coincidence. Me too."

After we miraculously agreed, we mostly ate our meals in silence. Come to think of it, silence didn't feel awkward with her. I might even call it normal.

"Mmm."

Hinami popped a piece of mackerel into her mouth. Man, she looked just as good eating Japanese food as Western. Whether she was picking off a piece of fish with her chopsticks and putting it in her mouth or lifting her bowl to elegantly sip her miso soup, she was always beautiful. Even the rice she picked up between her chopsticks seemed to glisten more brightly than other rice.

"...What?"

"Oh yeah."

As she stared back at me, I remembered something else I wanted to do today. I pulled the black backpack she'd temporarily given me out of my nerdy old bag.

"The reason we got together today was so I could return this, right?" I said with a hint of irony.

She snorted. "What, you don't want it anymore? If you plan to keep trying to beat this game, you might as well keep it. It's frayed anyway, so I wouldn't use it."

She popped another piece of mackerel into her mouth.

"No, I'll give it back. I'm going to buy a similar one with my own money… I'd rather do that, actually."

"…Is that so?" She took the bag I was holding out and spread it between both hands. As she looked for the frayed section, she smiled a little. "You're silly," she muttered.

"Silly? I thought you'd call me a genius."

I'd neatly covered the little worn patch with the fireworks pin she'd returned to me on the platform.

"I'm giving both of them back to you," I said bluntly, taking a sip of tea. She poked at the pin.

"You're giving the backpack *and* the pin back? But this was supposed to be an exchange for the bag."

"Don't worry about it."

I wanted to get across my genuine feelings, so I continued.

"It's just a small token of thanks for making my world more colorful."

I wanted to look away out of embarrassment, but I didn't.

She blinked a few times without saying anything, then mumbled, "Really?" She flicked the pin with her fingertips. "If that's the case, then I'll take it."

She smiled. On one corner of her backpack, a little firework exploded brilliantly, bringing color to the pitch-black world.

Afterword

Happy New Year. It's me, Yuki Yaku.

I'm overjoyed that the *Bottom-Tier Character Tomozaki* series has finally reached Volume 3, which I've heard is a threshold in many senses. Thanks entirely to the support from all my readers, it looks like I'll be able to continue with future volumes as well.

I've thought seriously about what I can do to repay the favor, as well as what I need to tell myself right now, and as you may have already guessed, I've concluded there's just one answer.

It has to do with the very subtle transparency of Kikuchi-san's button-down shirt in the illustration on the front cover.

The first thing I'd like you to look at is the shadow on her right sleeve, which would be her left sleeve from her own perspective. Observe that this is not a shadow expressing the wrinkles in her clothing or the cast of the light but rather a shadow whose purpose is to reveal her shirt's transparency by following the line of her arm.

Of course, the perfectly Kikuchi-san-like delicacy of this arm, as well as the powerful way in which the illustrator inspires the protective instinct through the use of transparency, are truly impressive. But what touches my heart most deeply is a fact that becomes apparent only through comparison with the first and second volumes.

I urge those of you who have a copy of the first or second volume at hand to have a look for yourself. I think you'll see that in those illustrations, the button-down shirts worn by Hinami-san and Mimimi are not transparent.

At first, I didn't grasp the meaning behind this difference, but when I finally did, it was like a blow to the head.

This is the difference between summer and winter fabrics.

The button-down shirts in the first two volumes have long sleeves, which means they are meant for winter. Therefore, the fabric is thicker and does not reveal their skin. But in the third volume, the button-down shirts have short sleeves made from thinner fabric, so the skin underneath becomes visible.

This subtle difference gives rise to a cover filled with real power. Not only did it make me, the very person who wrote the characters in this book, ask myself if I'd ever thought about the fabric their button-down shirts were made from, but it also raised the issue of what the material of a button-down shirt truly represented for me.

And now on to the acknowledgments.

To Fly-san, my illustrator. For everything from the illustrations in this volume to the special gift, thank you. Let's keep making *sashimi* our keyword as we continue on this project together. I'm a fan.

To Iwaasa-san, my editor. You made it through the hellish year-end rush. Thank you. It really was hellish, wasn't it?

Finally, to all my readers. Thank you for reading my books and supporting my work. Although I don't always reply, I do read your messages and letters, and I am truly grateful for them.

I hope you'll join me for the next volume.

Yuki Yaku